BEYOND TERRA

A NOVELLA IN THE FLOW OF POWER

R.V. JOHNSON

The Flow Of Power

The Flow of Power Chronicles:
Beyond the Sapphire Gate
Beyond the Dark Gate
Beyond Astura
Beyond High Reach

R.V. Johnson has had the worlds of the *Beyond* series hovering in his thoughts for many seasons. *Beyond Terra* slipped in while writing *Beyond the Sapphire Gate*, and *Beyond the Dark Gate*.
For author updates and a free copy of *Beyond the Sapphire Gate*, visit https://www.authorrvjohnson.com

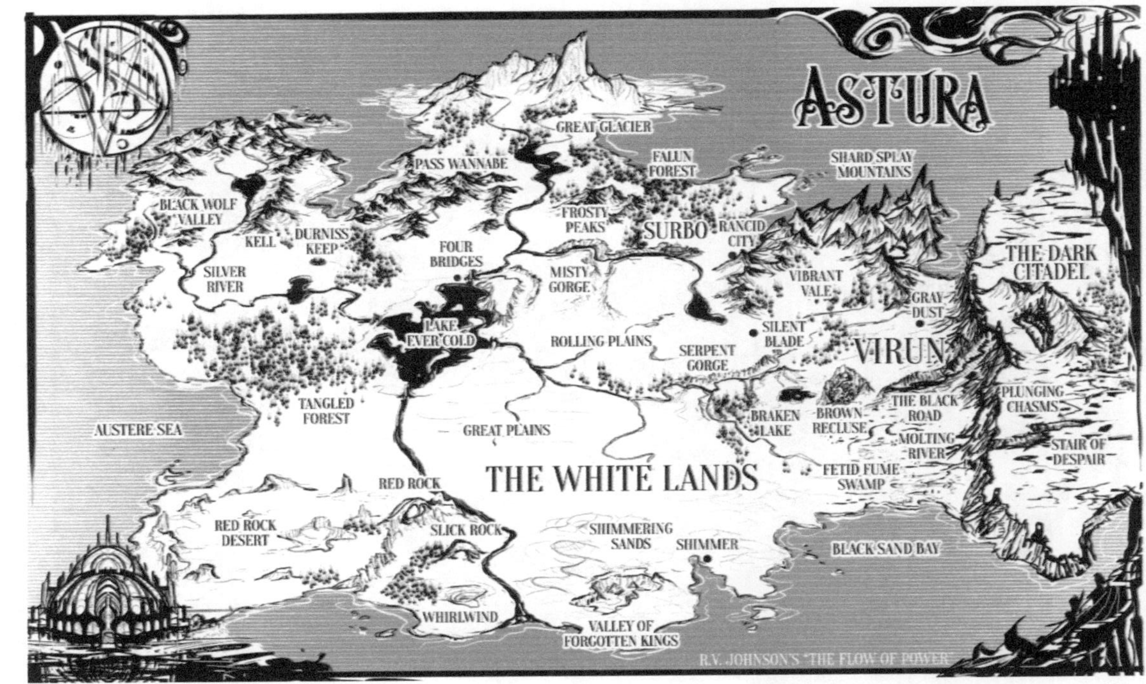
ASTURA
GREAT GLACIER
PASS WANNABE
FALUN FOREST
SHARD SPLAY MOUNTAINS
BLACK WOLF VALLEY
FROSTY PEAKS
SURBO
RANCID CITY
KELL
DURNISS KEEP
FOUR BRIDGES
MISTY GORGE
VIBRANT VALE
THE DARK CITADEL
SILVER RIVER
GRAY DUST
LAKE EVER COLD
ROLLING PLAINS
SILENT BLADE
VIRUN
SERPENT GORGE
TANGLED FOREST
BRAKEN LAKE
BROWN RECLUSE
THE BLACK ROAD
PLUNGING CHASMS
AUSTERE SEA
GREAT PLAINS
MOLTING RIVER
STAIR OF DESPAIR
FETID FUME SWAMP
RED ROCK
THE WHITE LANDS
RED ROCK DESERT
SLICK ROCK
SHIMMERING SANDS
SHIMMER
BLACK SAND BAY
WHIRLWIND
VALLEY OF FORGOTTEN KINGS
R.V. JOHNSON'S "THE FLOW OF POWER"

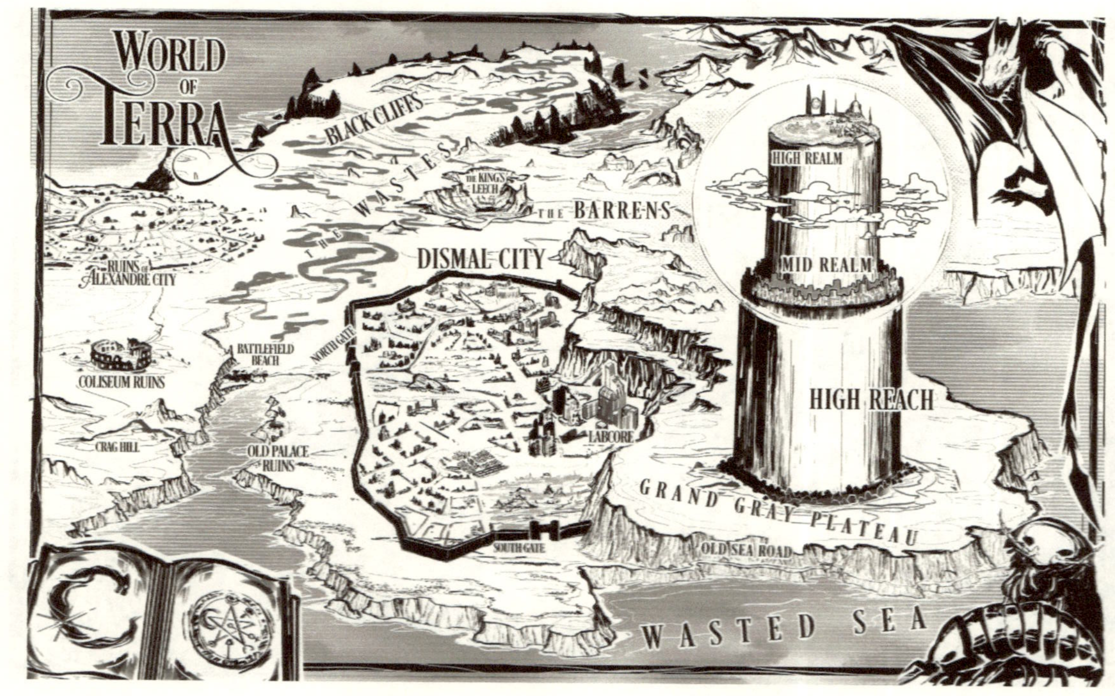

WORLD OF TERRA
BLACK CLIFFS
THE WASTES
THE KING'S LEECH
THE BARRENS
DISMAL CITY
RUINS OF ALEXANDRE CITY
COLISEUM RUINS
BATTLEFIELD BEACH
CRAG HILL
NORTH GATE
OLD PALACE RUINS
LABCORE
SOUTH GATE
OLD SEA ROAD
GRAND GRAY PLATEAU
HIGH REACH
MID REALM
HIGH REALM
WASTED SEA

CONTENTS

Chapter One

Isopod

The mountain plateau had a name once, long ago when the air was breathable, before one had to supplement one's blood with oxygil capsules. Crawling up it like a bug, Trenton Bonner was one of the few who knew it used to be just a mountain instead of the hybrid tower thing that it was now. PallTech had researched the mountain's past and somehow learned the original name given it of High Reach. Before gaining his legs, Trenton couldn't have cared less. Now he had no choice. He couldn't get it out of his mind if he wanted; the speed memory programs in the isolation cubes had done the job too well.

At the base of the High Reach, he'd scaled steep granite that rose vertically for a thousand steps to a monumental plateau. From there, the synthesized plasicrete, considered harder than crystal granite and indestructible, wrapped around the natural rock to form a giant tower. It began again on the next plateau higher, rising above Mid Realm and on up to High Realm way above the pollution.

As he climbed, Trenton appreciated how dragging his useless lower body around for so long had strengthened his arms and chest, which helped him now. When Pall-Tech had contacted him offering an experimental chance to walk without the need for costly robotic legs, he'd agreed with minimal convincing. A living protein gel chip implanted in his spine and receiving instructions from his brain seemed a risk worth taking.

As an added benefit—which the med techs hadn't foreseen—the cellular injections had increased his entire body's bone density and muscle mass. He was happy to have the enhancements, and when the hidden corporation had informed him of the conditions for their service beforehand, he hadn't balked. Who would turn down new legs in exchange for climbing a mountain to heist equipment needed to save lives? Some of those lives were his friends, not to mention his own.

Low Realm was running out of time, and possibly Mid Realm and High Realm too, though they might never admit it. Things, dark things, had swooped and crawled out of the pollution.

Dara. Trenton would not let himself dwell on her sudden death. He could not. She'd meant too much to him in the short time they'd worked together.

Again, Trenton activated the ion laser cutter mechanically grafted to the longest finger on his right hand and then melted an oblong handhold in the plasicrete wide enough for his boot. Waiting a moment for it to cool, he slipped his hand inside, protected mostly by his grip-enhanced rockprene gloves.

This high up, the frigid air cooled everything quickly, making him glad to have a climate-controlled suit. Even though its imprinted circuitry made him believe he'd stand out like some overgrown electronic creature, the odds of anyone spotting him were low. The only moving crafts at this level were zip cycles and the occasional cargo hovercraft. So far, he'd been able to hang motionless and camouflaged, the suit as close to the blue-green color of plasicrete as PallTech could make it.

Trenton burned another hole, waiting less time for it to cool. His palm grew warm through the glove, though not uncomfortably so. Trenton gained a small amount of satisfaction from the knowledge that faster cooling would speed his upward progress, though not as much as he'd like.

Pulling his feet into the melt holes his hands had recently vacated, Trenton gathered his bearings. The glint of something moving above caught his eye. According to intelligence reports, it was too early into the climb to encounter the bio-guardians. But when were the blasted reports ever right? If he hoped to keep enough heat to get to the dome alive and without frostbite, he had to keep moving.

The red Incoming Transmission button lit up on his wrist as he stretched for the next higher burn hole. He nearly lost his grip on the Mountain. Hugging the wall, he thumbed the button to activate the translink. "What is it, Pall?"

"You are overdue for a checkpoint, and your heart rate spiked, but it is back to normal now," Katy said, the tone of her voice only slightly scolded. Her voice was still crisp and clear. This high up, it surprised him how well the transmission came through.

Trenton was glad Katy had monitored the translink on a second shift.

"I ran into a slight snag. The bio-guardians are lower than reported."

Trenton could almost hear the blip of Katy's heart rate spiking on her instrument screens.

"Are you going to have enough oxygil capsules to go around them?" Katy asked. "We calculated those precisely with the rest of your carry weight."

"I was hoping you could tell me. The guardians are only two stories higher, and I still cannot see the dome."

"Stand by."

Trenton burned another hold, pulling his lean, muscular body higher as the cold crept inside. The climate suit was failing, the climb taking longer than PallTech had calculated. Standing by had become something he could no longer afford.

Trenton made it a full story before the transmission light flashed again. "What do we know?"

"From your current... You moved again, recalculating. From your present position, there are eighty-four stories left to climb, requiring forty-two capsules. You have forty-four remaining."

"Forty-three, I used two during a bout of lightheadedness."

"I'm not sure that matters. Your suit can no longer maintain your required body temperature with any efficiency. You have a higher probability of dying from hypothermia and frostbite."

"Thanks for the encouragement. I really needed it. Is there something else you wish to chat about, or should I keep moving?"

"Why are you hanging around? You should get going. Contact will occur next, should you reach the dome. There is one last thing."

"What is it?

"May luck climb with you. Katy out."

After working methodically for six bells, Trenton rested, looking at the horizon. The sun had dropped considerably. Once it did, the temperature would plummet, and there wasn't enough energy stored in the suit's heat cells to warm him through another frigid night.

After already climbing for three days and two nights, Trenton despaired he would never make it to the top. He'd die clinging to the Mountain until his fingers broke off and his frozen, ice slab of a body fell...

Trenton continued upward and met his first bio-guardian crawling down toward him. PallTech had little knowledge about them, only that the human-created isopods fed on pollutants growing on the plasicrete. Whether the isopods attacks on humans were unknown, though he suspected it. The king's administration would have bred them for other abilities, such as raising an alarm, an aggressive obstacle, or both.

Trenton was about to find out. The isopod had not deviated from its chosen path, tramping close enough for him to get a good look at it. With its multitude of legs, it moved slowly, but it kept a firm grip on the plasicrete with more than half of them. Smacking it off the Mountain would not work, even if he had a weapon; its hold was stronger than his was. The isopod's translucent carapace sparkled with irregular flashes of blue electricity.

Never altering its pace, the isopod reached him. Trenton activated the cutter on his free hand, intending to scare it away, but the creature charged into it, finally halting as it burst into flames of brilliant blue.

Leaning away from the oblong ball of flames as far as he dared, Trenton kept his fragile grip on the Mountain.

The isopod burned quickly, generating an intense heat as the crackling flames shrank fast. Silent except for a random pop and a few crackles, the isopod relinquished its grip and fell past him.

Trenton hung in place for a while, listening to his thumping heartbeats and going over in his mind what he'd just found out about the bio-guardians. The isopods' bio cells were flammable and their vision was poor; the thing had not seen him right until its impact with the cutter.

Had its demise caused an alarm? If security hovers suddenly converged on his position, he'd have the answer. For now, he may as well keep moving; the heat from the pod was already fading.

There was a benefit to the bio isopods, perhaps a lifesaving one. They packed a heat source.

For the next two bells, Trenton's world became a deadly game: burn hand- and footholds, climb as fast as possible, fry an isopod, and then absorb all the heat he could before it suddenly dropped, taking him along. He had so many narrow escapes he lost count.

Finally, Trenton looked up to see the bottom of the dome, a mere three stories away, though it might as well have been a hundred. His grip had dwindled to tingling fingers and shaky arms. Even his en-hanced legs were cramping, and now that he'd stopped moving, the cold fell upon him as thick as a hover pallet slab of ice, bringing on the shivers.

The translink lit again. Reaching for it, he hesitated. Bright in the darkening night, he swept the flashing beam back and forth. No isopods around when he needed them. He must've destroyed all those nearby. What should he do? He struggled harder to think; his mind was growing lethargic from the cold. Trenton had two options—somehow keep moving or die. But he was tired, weary past the point of caring. Trenton stared at the red light, wondering what to do about it. The flashes were getting annoying. Then he recalled he could press it.

"Trent!"

"Yes, who is this?"

"Katy, of course, but don't worry about that now. Your blood oxygen level has dropped to nearly sixty-eight percent; the oxygen air saturation is close to ten percent. I need you to listen carefully and do exactly what I ask. Put your free hand on your right thigh."

"What? Why?"

"Just do it!"

"Oh, sorry, I have done it."

"Lift the flap on your pocket, reach inside, and grab an oxygil capsule. Can you do that?"

"I think so, but I'm tired."

"Do it now, Trenton. Don't make me angry."

"Okay, got it."

"Pinch it between your thumb and forefinger. Put it up your nose this time. Hurry!"

"Okay."

"We have no time for the scheduled dosage to be released into your bloodstream. You may feel lightheaded at first. Let's hope you don't black out."

"I feel sick."

"Don't vomit! That may eject the capsule."

"Okay, you don't have to get mad."

"Is your mind still fuzzy?"

"That was a kind of odd thing to say."

"Was it? Do me a favor and put another capsule in your other nostril."

"If you say so," Trenton said, pinching the capsule and putting it where she wanted. Surprisingly, his hands no longer tingled. Some of his weariness had also dropped away like a falling isopod.

"That's better. Your level is at seventy-seven percent and climbing. Why haven't you been taking them?"

"Haven't I? I guess I've been busy trying to keep from freezing to death."

"Is blacking out and falling a better death? I think you're almost to the second obstacle."

"Second?"

"Yeah. The first was the Mountain itself."

"Oh, right. The dome is visible. I'm going to cut through while I still have the strength. I will initiate contact once inside."

"Okay. Watch for hovercraft."

"I will. Katy?"

"Yes?"

"Thanks for keeping me breathing for a little longer."

"You're welcome, but you owe me, and I intend to collect. PallTech out."

Trenton wondered how much she meant it.

Chapter Two

Curtain of Darkness

Twelve handholds brought him within reach of the dome. The dome's radial curve overlapped the bottom of the first plateau nearly a story, as if the Mountain's tower had pierced a fallen, translucent moon to its core.

The dome's surface had an odd, speckled appearance to it as if pitted with large holes, but Trenton felt no indents while rubbing his gloved hand over the surface. Cutting into it required a different tool. Switching hands, he freed his left one and pulled the gem cutter out from his suit's front.

Despite his slow, clumsy movements, the titanium diamond wheels cut two strips out of the bottom without too much effort. Alarmed at his deteriorating condition to the cold, he changed his original entry plan and cut a circle instead of a square, pushing the rounded piece to one side and leaving it leaning on the inside of the dome's overlap.

As he watched, a portion grew back on the circle. The bio-repair cells were working at closing the gap faster than the brains at PallTech had anticipated, making it a tight fit already.

Trenton scrambled to squeeze through, experiencing a moment of panic when his feet slipped out of the burn holes, but spreading his elbows beyond his circular entry stopped his fall. Pulling his legs up, he straddled the hole and stood. From there, the plateau's lip was within easy reach. He pulled himself the rest of the way up and then took a last look at his entry.

The hole shrank fast; the piece he'd cut and set against the dome's curvature had nearly absorbed into the shell. It was time to get moving. The dome would've sent a message to the core by now with the details of the breech. With luck, it would not generate a high-priority request; the urgency would depend on parameters like oxygen loss, length of time since the puncture, and how many reconstruction cells it had used, providing the briefing PallTech presented had had a grain of truth to it.

Trenton suspected the informant they re-lied upon had left some things vague, per-haps to retain enough value to remain alive. Trenton wasn't positive, but he felt PallTech would cross any boundary in their efforts to succeed with this mission—their survival and that of half the planet depended on it. In any event, a dome inspector would surely come soon.

Trenton set out for the plateau's interior, feeling his body temperature rise with exer-tion. He tapped the blinking translink.

Katy's voice, surrounded by the static in-herent to the biosphere, was scathing. "Why have you failed to respond? Your body tem-perature dropped way into the red zone."

"Everything is fine. I'm inside Mid Realm and at the halfway point. Now all I have to do is climb to High Realm without a patrol spotting me."

"You owe me a shot of rye for that. Don't get too exuberant, the worst may still lie ahead. Stay alert."

"Yes, my lady Katy."

"I've told you not to call me that. One other thing, Bonner."

"What?"

"Check in at the agreed-upon intervals and don't get hurt. You owe me a drink."

"Technically, that's two things. Three if you count the drink later."

"Just do it. Katy out."

Taking a last look around to ensure he was clear, Trenton cut a hole in the pla-sicrete wall of the first plateaued step of Mid Realm. At least, he thought of them as plateau steps. In reality, they were giant landings as the tower rose higher.

Trenton hoped none of the outer rim patrols would notice the gaping black dots climbing uniformly up the hard, blue-green substance. He'd kept them as small as he safely could, but he had a feeling that was too much to ask for. If all went well, the administration's security would cordon off Mid Realm and waste time looking for him. Trenton intended to hide in plain sight. Well, above it, at least.

Once he topped the first and largest plateau, Trenton climbed a high plasicrete wall, slipped down a small stairway, and sprinted across an illuminated transport flight path. He sighed with relief when he made it to the shadows of several spare cargo containers. Most gaped open to dispel the smell of previous freight. Whatever was stored in them was strong enough to make him gag. Trenton hurried past. Uniform housing, each looking the same as the one beside it, spread beyond the containers. If PallTech's intelligence was correct, he'd have them for cover all the way to the center of the realm.

Midway through the night, Trenton made it to the next—and last—plateau, and then checked in with his favorite, feisty tech.

"Our selected route seemed too easy. At least, moving across Mid Realm has. I've reached the last plateau without incident. Is something going on with the king and the administration?"

There was a slight delay from the dome's interference, and then Katy's voice crackled in his ear. "Our illustrious king and his administrators' only concern is that the realms beneath them to do as they command. They control what little we eat and believe themselves impenetrable inside their magnificent dome high upon their mighty tower. They're not, but don't get too confident; the worst is ahead of you."

Trenton was well aware how little proper food trickled down to Low Realm, but he hadn't wanted to interrupt. Listening to Katy's lovely, vibrant voice for days on end would not pose a problem, particularly as he crossed such a dangerous and desolate realm. "What can I expect from this last hurdle? Then again once I reach the tower?"

"The organic isopods are more numerous, though there's an unsubstantiated report the scurries' instincts make them want to bask in the morning sun after a night of cold. They may gather on the east side at first. PallTech recommends a slight course deviation to begin on the west."

"'Scurries,' so that's what you call them. I agree with the route change. Send it to me, please."

"The transmission is already in route."

"Thought so. You're just too good."

"We'll see when you return. Your energy is running low. Have you taken the allotted nutrient capsule?"

"They have no taste."

"Trent!"

Trenton laughed quietly and then swallowed, washing a capsule down with the last of his filtered water as he crept forward. The great plasicrete tower loomed above everything, taking up most of the upper plateau. He'd have to refill somewhere if he lived longer than a day.

"Nutrient capsule taken and new course plotted. This is goodbye until I reach the target point."

"Watch what you're doing. I don't want to come in there after you. The dome is so artificial, it gives me the creeps."

"So far, those things slinking out of the Wastes in Low Realm are worse than anything encountered up here. If everything goes as planned, I'll be back to fight them for you before you know it."

"You'd better. They're getting bolder and you still owe me that drink...at your place. End of translink."

Trenton smiled. Katy was getting good at flirting, though they both knew that was all it would ever amount to. Her seventeen seasons, eight less than his, put her in the realm of a little too young for him. Though it took some of the tension from the mission, which was probably what she had intended.

Trenton strode up to the ever-rising tower, slowly gaining height as it moved toward the roof of the organic biosphere that expanded as the terraformed platform ascended from the plasicrete poured under it daily. He set to work cutting handholds.

The plotted route proved a good one; he only had to dispatch the occasional robotic-organic bug. The scurries moved sluggishly out of the western darkness toward the grayness growing in the east. Most of them moved straight east, forgoing their usual zigzag scouting pattern, allowing him to climb unhindered for the rest of the night.

When early morning light filtered in, revealing that his destination was not so far away, everything changed for him as his excitement rose. He couldn't believe he'd made it this far. PallTech probably couldn't either.

Enormous bugs meandered along the top rim. Hovercraft hung motionless just below them, or moved leisurely around the tower on a set flight path. Large, wheeled troop carriers made of some shiny metal rolled around the tower's perimeter, pulled by the biggest scurries he'd yet to see.

He thought about moving halfway down and attempting a quick translink with Pall-Tech for contingency routing advice, but there was no time. Two of the bigger isopods, carrying their enormous metal carapaces atop their endlessly moving legs, broke off from the crowd at the rim and began moving down. To the side, a two-seater zip cycle cruised his way. Trenton froze. The isopods were taking their time, shuffling about on the tower, but the zip cycle would reach him soon. He had to remain motion-less and hope his suit's camouflage kept prying eyes from discovering him.

He did not have to wait long. Slightly be-low him, the cycle drifted lazily around the tower. A man and a woman dressed in the uniform of the administration's militia sat upon the two seats, the man seated behind the woman who guided the craft in its slow orbit.

The woman gazed outward and for-ward from time to time, while the man looked down. Trenton held his breath, his palms sweaty beneath his gloves. The cycle thrummed by, the idling thrust motor loud in his ears. Just a few more seconds and it would pass. Trenton breathed easier.

The woman glanced up, staring right at him. Reacting on instinct, Trenton let go of his handholds and dropped onto the seat too close behind the man, knocking him hard to one side. The man's arm flailed about, grasping for the stabilizer railing mounted on the side of the front seat, but he had already fallen past.

Trenton turned to the woman and found a cell disruptor leveled at him held by steady hands, though her oval brown eyes were wide. Seasons of hard training had conditioned him: he dived for the railing the man had missed. Getting a firm grip, he swung his legs into open air, coming at her from the side with both feet extended. His feet connected.

Kicked away from the cycle, the woman slammed hard into the tower with a grunt, but she kept the disruptor's wide barrel raised and pointed at him. He dove to the back seat as the red, luminous beam flashed across the steering bar. Sliding, the woman fell from sight.

Like the man, no scream passed her lips.

As he climbed to the front seat, Trenton briefly regretted their fate. They were simply at the wrong place at the wrong time, when there was no choice but for him to take their lives or he'd lose his.

The woman had taken the control device with her' there was likely a transmitter attached to her somewhere. He would have to control it manually with a considerable portion of the cycle's maneuverability corrupted. Part of the top half of the manual steering bar was molten metal.

The isopods were distraught, moving back and forth and climbing over the top of each other as they crawled down the tower toward Trenton. They must have gotten his scent or smelled the fear of the falling militia. Pushing the steering rod forward, Trenton sped up, going higher. The zip cycle's handling was awkward, forcing him to bend too far forward, but it would have to do.

The top of the Mountain was close. High Realm came into view and spots of green foliage stood out against the plasicrete landings and roadways covered by domes within the dome.

As Trenton topped out, a heavily guarded convoy of transport hovers and large transport isopods moved in single file ahead. A glance in both directions revealed militia patrols—on the ground and in hovers—coming toward the slower caravan.

Trenton steered close to a pair of single-rider zip cycles trailing behind the convoy, matching their speed. The two men controlling the cycles looked back, but did not seem concerned. They returned their attention to the cultivated fields, sparse dwellings, and the Mountain tower's edge, only glancing back at Trenton occasionally.

His brash ruse worked for now, but the two bodies in Mid Realm would raise alarms. Slowly, Trenton let the cycles expand the distance between him and them. Veering off when he judged it time, he zipped toward the center of High Realm, only looking back once. No one followed, much to his relief.

Trenton flew past orchards of real fruit trees and factories that pumped out synthetic proteins, and over lightning beam fences caging cloned horses and animals unknown to him; none had populated the planet in his lifespan.

Though he felt the need to hurry, he slowed slightly to get a better view; he'd always wanted to see animals. Any animal, it didn't matter. Perhaps someday he'd get to touch them with his bare hands, feel their fur against his fingers and palms.

The wooly, white-furred animals huddled together in the center of their smaller field, and large feline and canine animals patrolled the laser-beamed fences on opposite sides, their eyes fixed on the huddlers. Smaller gray- and red-furred creatures gazed with interest on the remaining two sides.

Trenton sympathized with the white fur balls. They reminded him of his former life with no legs and his struggle for survival in Low Realm. He could still hear the words of disdain spoken by those who passed him when he begged near the Wastes. "Bent

Bonner, cannon fodder," they said, their voices oddly distorted behind their rad filter masks, though it was theoretical whether the masks helped. Back then, he hadn't been able to afford one, and so far, he hadn't contracted the skewed skin some of those with the masks had.

Trenton throttled the zip cycle, zooming at full speed, and the wind pressed against his face and roared in his ears. He would have smiled if he could have opened his lips. It was exhilarating. The great palace and the grand administration buildings grew larger on the horizon. The translink lit on his arm.

Trenton slowed enough to hear and speak and then acknowledged the transmission. "What is it? The next scheduled communication was at the destination. My estimated arrival is three-point-five minutes."

"Two-point-eight minutes at your current speed," Katy's voice blared into his ear. The irritation in the volume of her tone was unmistakable. "What are you doing? Militia is bound to investigate your lengthy thrust signature. Are you trying to get caught?"

Veering slightly south, he slowed. Katy was right, as usual. "I suppose I must slow it down. Sorry about that. I got somewhat carried away."

"Somewhat? The team here has a running bet you tried to break a speed record. You're a little short. I suggest you save the next try for when the militia comes after you."

"Do they realize there are no pollutants here, causing excess drag from the thicker air down there? I could probably do it, at least compared to the records of Low Realm."

"Hilarious. I'm certain such great minds would've considered that little fact. They've spent seasons hearing the hoarse sounds of their breathing when outdoors," Katy said. "Though I wonder why everyone here at control has suddenly gotten quiet."

Trenton chuckled. "Let them contemplate it for a while. How far is it now?"

"One-point-five minutes. Watch for the glint of the private dome. I'm surprised you haven't already seen it. This one rivals those of the palace and the administration buildings."

A rainbow-colored hue above a high wall made from stone was Trenton's only warning. He swerved at the last second. "Whoa! Why is this dome so transparent?"

"From the extravagant fact that it's a variation of plasicrete, not a bio-structure. Take a few seconds to locate the target entry and hover there. Don't touch the wall! That structure has heat and tremor alarming. The person who designed the security was good but didn't know cutting through pla-sicrete would be possible. Back then, it wasn't. Cut through the dome and drop down."

"What if I hadn't come across a zip cycle?"

"I'd have plotted another entrance. This is better. Contact will occur next once you're inside. Katy out."

A slow cruise around the back of the dome took him away from the heavier traffic area of his arrival, which showed signs of increasing morning activity. An open field lay behind, separating several other structures. There was no glint of a dome covering them, and nothing moved around them, making patrols of the area less. Trenton set the cycle to hover above the wall.

Dropping to his stomach on the floor of the craft, Trenton reached down and cut a round hole in the dome, letting it fall upon a spongecrete pad between two blocky stat-ues.

Thinking to hang from the cycle's bottom foot rails, Trenton got on his knees with his legs dangling outward.

Etched on a button underneath the seat, a symbol signified a cable lift. As he pressed it, a trapdoor opened in the foot rail and a buttoned rectangular hook on a cable lowered almost down to one statue. Smiling, he retracted it by pressing it again, halting it where he wanted it with another press. Clasping the hook to the ring built on his suit at his abdomen, he slipped over the edge rail. Holding onto the cable with one hand, he pressed the hook's button.

The cable halted near an isopod-shaped statue realistically displayed with its scissor-like mandibles spread. Releasing the hook, Trenton dropped onto its carapace and shimmied down a leg to the ground.

The target was finally in sight. Or rather, two of the targets sat hulking side by side outside a large warehouse. Trenton moved toward the huge transport hovers. Choosing the one closest gave him the best chance security would not spot him. His translink lit. He pressed the response button immediately, keeping his voice low. "I haven't cleared the target of hostiles yet; make it fast."

"Stop," Katy said.

Trenton froze. "Huh? Have I been compromised?"

"Not yet. We have new information. Your first target is inside the warehouse."

"Is that wise? A place this secure would have an elaborate alarm system built into the dome. High Realm security is likely already on their way."

"No one raised the alarm, or we'd know it."

Trenton knew surprise.

"The warehouse should pose little hindrance for someone with your training," Katy added, her voice sullen. "Contact will occur when you're inside. Katy out."

Trenton ground his teeth. He didn't like it. As it stood, if he left right now, he had a good chance of getting away once he'd retrofitted the cutter onto one of the robotic arms on the hover transport as he'd planned.

Trenton slipped around the two craft, hoping they were unmanned. If they weren't, the pilots had seen him by now, anyway.

The retractable dock door had an ion beam for security. Tricky to bypass even on his best days, much less after five solid days of climbing. Striding past the dock door, he spotted the faint traces of the beam leaking around a barely discolored wall section the size of a small window. Trenton swore. His physical stats had scanned to a holofeed.

The need for stealth gone, Trenton walked boldly to an old buzz-me-in door he had only read about as part of PallTech's briefing on the man who had set up the dome's security. Garnet Creek had favored a mixture of old technology with new.

The door proved easy, pushing open when he cut the lock off, gaining him entry into a windowless foyer. Cutting the inner door the same way, Trenton kept the cutter hot for the guards awaiting his entry into the warehouse dock. He pulled the door open and dove behind a cargo container.

Peering around it, Trenton frowned, feeling slightly foolish. The room was devoid of life and motion. He released the cutter's ignition lever, letting the flame extinguish as the blade retracted into his extended finger. He pressed the translink. "The rear dock is empty. I don't suppose the new target is lying somewhere around here beckoning me with flashing lights to come pick it up?"

"Hardly. Find the neural scan door and show us your expertise. Get past it without raising an alarm. Beyond it is a storage area with antigravity shelves, the only ones in the building. Go through them to the stainless-steel vault. The target is farther inside. The next transmission will occur there. You're getting close."

"Wait! Is this worth such an enormous risk? What is it?" Trenton asked, but the translink had already gone dark.

Trenton felt like mashing his thumb against the button and yelling his questions into the ears of all those sitting in the cramped little room hidden below Low Realm. Katy sat there, giving and receiving suggestions from scientists old enough to have parented her, and who mingled with techno-brains barely older than his flirtatious prodigy.

Instead, he moved on. He was wasting precious time thinking about the way Pall-Tech operated, a habit he needed to curb. He wasn't crawling along the Wastes wondering where he was going to get his next oxygil capsule, not anymore. Just so long as he did what PallTech wanted.

The neural door was easy to discover. There was only one human-sized door accessing the warehouse interior from the rear dock. A red holo window, slightly larger than a human head, hovered in the air beside it, looking solemn and arrogant.

The scanner had a right to seem like that. Defeating it would require greater finesse than simply whipping out the cutter and blazing through the offending obstacle. Trying something like that would trigger the alarm and drop security doors in place.

So what could he do? Katy couldn't hack into the system and reprogram the scanner to recognize his neural cognizance or she would have done it already. This security must have a standalone network. Perhaps this was as far as he was going. Trenton reached for the translink and then paused. If he could not defeat it, perhaps he could go around it—through the wall.

Once again, the plasicrete cutter—one of Katy's and crew's slicker inventions—came through for him. Cutting a shoulder-width circular hole, he kicked the smoldering steel inside and then crawled through, carefully avoiding the heated edges. The device awed him. What kind of weapon might he have if PallTech had equipped five of his fingers with such a thing?

The room was what Katy had described, a storage area for the warehouse with antigravity shelves filled with precisely fitted containers. The shelving swallowed all space except a hallway leading deeper inside.

The cutter had sliced through a shelf along with the rounded container on it. A glint of red inside the canister caught his eye.

Trenton picked up a ruby, rounded naturally to an orb, and too big to wrap his hand fully around. The small sphere was...magnificent. As flawless as anything he had ever encountered.

He brought it close to his eyes, gazing into the depths of its pristine purity, marveling at the clarity of its many layers. Wonder rose in his mind. There was something at the center. Something dark moved at its heart, a sense of shadow, a black spot. The shadowed spot radiated raw power, a power that was aware of him even as he sensed it. There was neither malice nor a feeling of danger, only...affinity. The orb belonged with him.

A redness of a different hue pulled him away. His translink was flashing again. Trenton's annoyance rose, but he quickly quelled it. He wanted to get this mission over with and go back to Low Realm where he belonged. The best way to do that was to use the resources provided by PallTech to bring them what they wanted. "I'm past the neural blockade. Where do I go now?"

"Good. We wondered. Your blood pressure dropped dangerously low, though it returned to normal fast. Did you run into trouble?"

"If by 'trouble,' you mean having to cut through a steel wall, then yeah, I did."

"Go sparingly with the cutter; the energy stored in the gel cells is not unlimited. We want it back intact."

"Okay, Mother Katy, where is the target?"

"Our source places it at the warehouse center inside a stainless-steel vault called 'the mausoleum.'"

"Great! I'll eventually have an altercation with security. This place must have private guards with all the valuable stuff stored here."

"What are the valuables?" Katy asked.

Trenton regretted mentioning items of value. He should have expected her reaction; the operating costs supporting him on this mission alone must cost a small fortune in credits. Not for the first time, he wondered where PallTech got its funding. "I've spent too long in here as it is. We'll talk later."

"Wait! Just a brief—"

Using the orb gently to press the translink button, Trenton severed the link. He was relieved at the silence of his own thoughts. Katy would pester him for descriptions until he gave in. He set the translink to stealth mode and blocked her from flashing him.

Liking the feel of the orb's pleasant weight and smooth touch against his palm, Trenton left it in his hand as he made his way out of the room.

The next room would have felt cavernous if not for the huge stainless-steel vault looming in the middle of it. A large, dark-glassed area overlooked the mausoleum. Most of it that faced the steel vault lay broken or missing.

A glass-topped desk sat upon a peculiar floor of embedded metal masks, and several glass panels on a back wall inside the room showed live images from in and around the warehouse. Trenton did not like what he saw on two of the panels. A significant security force was mobilizing at the king's administration buildings and at the palace.

If they were coming after him—and it was highly probable they were—his plasicrete burns in the tower would lead them here before long.

Turning to the mausoleum, he cut through the great clasps that locked the door in place. Picking up a tattered piece of burlap sack, he wrapped the orb in it, put it in the front pocket of his pants, and then struggled to open the hydraulic door. He pushed it along its track until he had an opening large enough to squeeze through.

Artifacts, gilded jewelry, suits of armor, exquisite statues of precious stone, and much more lay neatly piled throughout the wide room. He had no time to gape. He sent a transmission: "I'm in the vault and we're out of leisure time. What am I after?"

"Look for two sapphire crystal obelisks six hands high." Katy's words seemed rushed. She'd likely heard the urgency in his voice. Easily seen, the obelisks stood a doorway apart at the rear.

Trenton strode to them. "Found them."

"Take them to the transporter and strap them in."

"Are they valuable?"

"More than you can imagine."

"Then you owe me," he muttered, reaching for one. He hesitated. The symbol of interlocking lines etched near the top of each obelisk had an odd magnetism about them. The orb thrummed with power and tugged his hand toward the obelisks with an insistence Trenton found unnerving.

He touched it to the symbol.

Red sparks exploded from the orb, throwing him backward a step. The symbols rotated. Two luminous lines of jagged blue shot from the obelisks and met in the center. A curtain of dark mist dropped to the floor beneath it. Inside, a swirling storm raged in a constant flux.

"What is it?" Trenton asked aloud, reaching for it. "So beautiful!"

"What's beautiful? Trenton be careful, we—"

The instant Trenton touched the black curtain, his world changed.

CHAPTER THREE
CRIMSON ORB

AN OPULENT BEDROOM FILLED Trenton's vision. Someone slept in a silk-covered bed larger than his entire living cubicle. He backed away, ready to leave the same way he'd arrived, except there was only solidity behind him. A glance over his shoulder revealed a wall. The sapphire obelisks and the mausoleum had vanished.

His confusion warred with concern as the bed's occupant sat up, staring at him. From the looks of her, she was his age and beautiful, even after first awakening from sleep.

"Might I inquire why you stand in my chambers and where you hail from, outlander?" The woman's lilting voice fit her smooth, light features and black hair. Her blue eyes regarded him with curiosity but no malice, though he wouldn't know if she were the mother of goodness or the queen of darkness. Low Realm had an abundance of malevolent women. Nearly all were love-ly—lovely and deadly.

There was only one exit, a door across the room, which made him wonder again how he'd ended up where he was. But did he really need to know? He should go before the woman called for security, if she hadn't already. Pushing away from the wall, Trenton strode toward the door with a casual air he didn't feel.

"What makes you believe I'm an out-lander?" he asked, attempting to keep her preoccupied.

The woman pulled the silken covers to the side and draped a bare, trim leg over the edge. "Garbed as you are, do you have to ask? What have you in your hand?" Drawing a sharp breath, she slipped from the bed to stand before him, her sheer gown revealing a body as beautiful as her face.

Trenton's face heated as he stared. Look-ing down, he opened his fingers. The magnif-icent red orb now pulsated with a crimson inner light.

The woman's delicate hand flew to her lips. "Great Mother! You have a glimmer orb artifact! I have only heard tales of such things." Her words were hushed.

"Is that what you call it?"

The woman looked at him sharply, a stray lock of her glossy black hair falling across an eye. An impatient toss of her head dislodged the offending strands. "Do you not know what you carry?"

Trenton closed his fingers around the orb and put it in his front leg pocket as the woman watched his every move. "I must go. Sorry to have bothered you, Miss...?"

"My name is Khiminay. Please tell me, what is yours?"

"Trenton. Call me Trent if you like. It is nice to meet you, but I have to leave." He took a step toward the door.

Khiminay's hand closed around his arm with surprising strength. "What is the hurry, Outlander Trent?" Moving in front of him, she sidled close.

Trenton felt the heat of her firm body through his climate suit. Or did he? Perhaps it was the suit adjusting for the room and he only imagined what he wanted to feel. Her lips parted with a small, coy smile, and her round blue eyes locked with his, inviting and lovely.

Strangely, flecks of red pulsed in a line across her corneas. He gazed deep into them, trying to understand their meaning.

After a time, her long eyelashes fluttered, and she stepped back, eyeing him with renewed interest. "You have no color flecks, so you really are an outlander. You've not used for long, or you are not a User at all. In the latter case, the orb is of little value to you. Which is it?"

Trenton stifled his growing annoyance and anxiety. Was she stalling him by uttering cryptic nonsense? If so, it was working. "I have delayed too long." He shoved past her. "Please accept my apologies for disturbing your rest."

"Wait!" Khiminay's voice was urgent.

Trenton paused with his hand on the door, intrigued. Some kind of light beam, red, crisscrossed the door diagonally and horizontally from the top and both sides. It faded and vanished as he watched.

Grabbing a white robe from the bed, Khiminay flung it over her shoulders. "I am coming with you."

"Why?" Trenton asked, confused. "I have no intention of staying in the warehouse. I'll find a way out without your help."

Now Khiminay looked confused. She frowned. "What warehouse?"

Trenton didn't bother to answer. Whatever game Khiminay was playing, it wouldn't work unless he stuck around. Flinging the door open, he stepped into a stone hallway and started along it, wondering when the warehouse had changed from plasicrete flooring to stone; white granite from the looks of it.

Khiminay strode companionably beside him, the slap of her bare feet thudding dully in his ears. She'd left the robe open at the front. Sunlight reflecting from skylights and glowing, clear crystals wired on the wall revealed more than she probably knew. Wait! The crystal shards on the wall emitted their own light.

Wondering what powered them, Trenton headed for one only to turn away; his primary focus was to find a transport craft. Heisting one was critical to his survival and the survival of his few remaining friends in the lower realms. The bloody sapphire obelisks had gotten him sidetracked for too long. PallTech would just have to live without them.

Khiminay spoke from beside him. "Where is it you wish to go? Perhaps I can show the way."

"Outside."

"Then we should take the left hall."

Trenton did not know if he could trust her, or even if he should, but his options were dwindling with every step. Again he knew surprise. Security hadn't caught up with him yet. How much time had passed since he'd seen them mobilizing?

The hallway went on for much longer than he'd expected. When an intersection presented him with a choice, he swung into the left branch as Khiminay had suggested without slowing.

"The double doors at the hall's end lead to the courtyard."

Trenton breathed a sigh of relief. The hover transports were in the courtyard. He'd just need to board one and power the cells. Khiminay would have to go back inside at that point. Did he want that? If she came with him, she could likely talk them past security, something far easier than cutting through the dome from the hole he had started. And Katy would like the energy saved from the cutter's power cell. Perhaps he would ask her to come along.

Pushing on the doors, Trenton strode through, letting his eyes adjust to the sunlight so he could search for the best route to the transport craft.

Trenton froze. A courtyard, nothing like he expected, met his view.

There was no translucent bubble. A blue sky with patches of white clouds drifted past a marvelous fountain where white- and yellow-robed people had gathered. Beyond the fountain, a city of towering stone spires and crenelated rooftops spread outward. In the distance, tiny people wandered past an arched entrance leading to the long walkway of the fountain.

Khiminay tied her white robe at the waist and joined him on the short, one-step landing leading out into the courtyard. "Beautiful, is it not?"

Perplexed, Trenton stared. "Where am I?"

Khiminay again looked at him sharply. "You do not know Surbo, the capital city of the White Lands? You truly are an outlander. Have you traveled through a gateway from elsewhere on Astura or another world?" Khiminay paused, watching him.

Trenton could only stare at her as his mind grappled with the enormity of her words. "I don't understand. Are you saying I have traveled to another world? How did I get beyond Terra?"

Khiminay smiled knowingly and then beckoned to the group at the fountain, already moving toward them to make haste. "I met such a one not long past who was not from my planet, an outworlder." Her attention fixed on him again, her brief smile sympathetic. "A woman passed through a travel gateway and into my world of Astura."

A white-haired, white-bearded man spoke first as the group stopped at the foot of the landing, though Trenton barely heard him. "An outlander, Khiminay?"

An old woman wearing a white dress instead of the white or yellow robes the others wore took him by surprise. Easily eight feet tall, she towered over everyone, but what startled him most were her glowing eyes of white that shone brightly, even at midday.

Khiminay laid a hand on Trenton's shoulder. "He has given his name as Trent. And he carries something I think you should see, Durandas. You and those here with the Circle of Light."

Durandas hopped upon the landing, his long white beard billowing below a face too young for his stark, white hair. "You have my interest."

Khiminay squeezed his shoulder. "Please, show them."

Trenton considered. Finding the orb at the warehouse, he had no notion who owned it, nor did he care. He had an...affinity toward it.

Merely showing it to them couldn't hurt. Still, Trenton felt a strong reluctance as he pulled it from his pocket and held it in his palm.

A collective intake of breath arose from the members of the Circle of Light.

"A crimson crystal artifact," Durandas whispered. "I had thought none survived the degradation during this War of a Hundred and One Seasons. We must study it!" He reached for it.

Trenton closed his fingers around it and drew back. "No one touches it!"

Durandas's left palm rose to face the ground. "I am saddened to hear you speak so and now have little choice. We must analyze the crimson orb." His right hand vanished inside a ball of white radiance matching the old woman's eyes.

Trenton gaped.

A clear tube extended from the glowing hand to the white marble landing they stood on. The stone faded to transparency. Underneath the feet of the white-robed man—who seemed to stand on air—a frothing river of white raged, flashing with brilliant hues of red. The white substance filled the tube.

"Durandas, what are you doing? Stop!" the towering woman screamed.

An astoundingly bright flash of white jolted Trenton to the core, filling him with excruciating pain and then blessed darkness.

CHAPTER FOUR

CIRCLE OF LIGHT

TRENTON WOKE TO THROBBING pain inside his skull. Ignoring it, he sat up slowly. The old woman with the radiant white eyes—so odd without corneas—sat at the foot of the enormous bed he occupied.

"The healers brought you to my chambers at my request after the...altercation with Durandas. I could not determine then if you would survive."

"Who are you? Why did Durandas attack me?"

"I am the Lore Mother, the oldest of my kind. We are the Valens. As for the attack, I have yet to discover the why behind it. Durandas has never done such a thing. While you recover, I shall look into the matter."

Trenton touched the empty pocket where the orb had been. "I'm coming with you."

The Lore Mother's luminous eyes dimmed a little. "The Circle of Light has come to an agreement. You are to petition the Circle for your release after full recovery, which I shall recommend for two days hence."

"Huh? What about the red orb?"

The Lore Mother stood, moving with a vigor that belied her apparent age. "The Circle has a high division amongst them over the ownership of the crystal artifact, though most are intent upon returning it to you. They meet again at sunset. Now healers wish to finish what I cannot. When you can walk, someone will show you to another room."

Trenton didn't hide the bitterness in his voice. "So visitors can expect harsh treatment here?"

The Lore Mother's mouth tightened. "For now. I shall order food and drink brought to you. Do you require more?"

Trenton shook his head.

"Farewell then. Warriors guard these chambers to avoid disturbing your mend. Know that I speak on your behalf." Though meant to convey comfort, the tone of her words sounded apprehensive. As she closed the door behind her, he heard the lock click into place.

Neither the door nor the room had a window. A chamber pot sat on the floor at the base of the bed. The climate suit took care of his bodily fluids for now, but its urithium-powered cell would run dry in days. PallTech's engineers had a limited supply of the precious metal that stored the energy.

The door opened. A man and a woman in white robes filed inside, followed by two men wearing suits of silver armor who positioned themselves beside the door. Broad swords hung prominently at their hips.

Trenton grew wary. He doubted his laser cutter would stand a chance against a swinging sword should it come to that.

"The Lore Mother requests your full heal," the woman stated. Her hair was the deepest yellow. Long and wavy, it fell below shoulder length. Her vivid, light blue eyes seemed genuine. "Have you experienced pain or weakness, Outlander Trenton?"

The white-robed man folded his arms into his wide sleeves. "Regardless of your response, we shall look." He had no visible hair, not even an eyebrow lined his forehead. His light blue eyes, rounded chin, and oval face resembled the younger woman in a way.

Trenton ignored the man's comment. "I have some weakness, likely caused when one of your people tried to kill me and stole my orb."

The Lore Mother drooped a little. "I do not know what is wrong with our First Light. Durandas sits the highest on the Circle, yet his action was that of an apprentice."

"That is not for us to judge, Daramay. The crimson artifact is likely a Dark User tool. You heard Durandas. A city besieged as we are by such a great army, spawned by the Dark Citadel, can take no chances," the hairless man declared.

"As you say, Master Healer Leven. Let us continue this discussion in the future." Her eyes never leaving his, Daramay sat beside him on the bed. "We shall have to touch you to complete the final stage. Is this acceptable?"

Trenton shrugged. "I am feeling fine, but you will not believe me, so do as you must."

Daramay smiled as she put her hand on his wrist. A slight, not unpleasant feeling of warmth emanated from the touch. A look of annoyance marred Master Healer Leven's face, though he quickly masked it. He grabbed her bare shoulder.

The warmth changed to an itch, not large enough to require a scratch, but subtly insistent. It demanded notice, though it faded almost as soon as it began. The woman removed her hand. Leven let go, a glare shining in his dark eyes. Daramay didn't seem to notice. Her wide eyes were upon him. "Outlander Trenton is fit enough to walk to new chambers, or jog if he so desires. The Lore Mother is stronger than she claims."

Trenton decided to not mention his suit had activated its repair program. Besides shielding him from infections and salving the burned areas, the suit had boosted his immune system with injections while repairing itself above fifty percent. Doing so had cost much of the remaining power cells, but there was no help for it. The suit was hard-wired to protect itself and assist the wearer where possible.

Daramay stood gracefully, looking at Leven. "The Circle awaits your report. I shall escort the outlander to his new quarters."

Leven's agate eyes hardened. Flinging the door open, which caused the guard on the left to scramble to the side, the healer left.

If Leven's brusque manner bothered Daramay, she gave no indication. "Outlander Trenton, come with me, please."

Trenton stood. "Trenton, please."

Daramay smiled. "As you wish."

Daramay led the way into a wide hall. The two guards followed close behind.

Passing three intersections, Daramay unlocked a nondescript door.

Daramay spoke to the guards. "Please wait here. I believe we shall require an escort to the assembly hall soon."

"As you say, my lady," one guard said.

Trenton followed her into a smaller and less ornate single-person room. Inside, a small table and two chairs sat beside a bed not long enough to stretch his legs. He did not complain. There were many nights in Low Realm where his bed had comprised a plasicrete walkway.

"This way," Daramay said, passing through the bedroom and going into a room off to one side. A narrow pit in the floor contained pooled water flowing in from a hole in the granite stone at the top and out a trench at the bottom. "Remove your garment. I shall bathe you. The Circle of Light shall require you to address them. Leven has informed them of your remarkable healing by now."

Trenton regarded her for a long moment. Then, feeling he could trust her, he did as she asked. Pressing in and then pushing the cover guard to one side of his right armpit, he tapped an audible sequence of harmonious sounds on the touchpad. The suit clicked. Magnetic links disengaged, starting at the back of his neck and working down to his groin. He stepped backward out of the legs, leaving it standing of its own accord, the gloves drooping slightly downward. In standby mode, the climate suit would conserve its power cells longer.

The water was warm as he stepped down into it, sitting on the last step. Daramay took a soft washcloth from the folded stacks on the small shelves of both sides of the room and knelt beside him. A small frown furrowed her smooth forehead above her thin, golden eyebrows. "I do not understand. You do not have the harsh scent of someone dressed too long in armor. Nor are there signs of flash burns from the Flow. Are you also a healer?"

Trenton thought about how to answer without giving away the climate suit's enhancements to the wearer. He had no way of knowing what these people would do with the knowledge; his own world would kill...—no, had killed for it. Many explanations crossed his mind, but in the end, he kept it simple. "I have trained myself to listen to the signs of my body and follow the instructions closely. My...garment removes excess odor."

"Then you are a healer," she said, rubbing his back and shoulders gently with the soft cloth.

If Daramay noticed his extended finger, she said nothing. Trenton submerged it in the water beside his leg. "In a way, I suppose so, though not as strong as you. You are quite good."

Scrubbing his chest, Daramay paused, lowering her eyes. "You are too kind. Please stand, so I may finish."

Trenton did so, feeling slightly uncomfortable as she worked her way downward in silence. Briefly, he wondered how she could see at all through the veil of her flowing, shiny hair. When she finally pulled away after rubbing his feet one at a time, he sat down quickly.

"Why are you here?" Daramay suddenly asked.

Trenton gazed into her light blue eyes for the longest time. Her long eyelashes blinked slowly once or twice, but she kept her eyes locked with his. "You people call me an 'outlander.' 'Outworlder' is a better description."

"I am aware of how Khiminay found you and where she found you...in her private quarters as she slept. Why did you choose her location?"

"I didn't choose a location. The orb dropped me there; at least I think it caused all this."

"The crimson orb may have the ability to travel. We know little about it. Only that it is a Dark User artifact, one particularly effective for one attuned as a Red."

"I'm not a Red, or at least I don't think so. I'm not quite certain what one is..."

"Red robes are congruous with the Dark Flow and the Dark Citadel, where most of the Dark Users live."

Trenton opened his mouth to ask her about the citadel, but another white-robed woman strode into the tiny room. A white stone gleamed dully on her forehead, secured there by a wide leather strap.

"What causes this interruption, Marnie?" Daramay asked.

"The Circle of Light is assembling. I am to help you get the outlander ready." Her light green eyes appraised him with every word she spoke. In one hand, the woman carried a nondescript gray robe. Setting the robe on a shelf of soft cloths, she picked a cloth up.

"The Circle does not condone delay. Please stand here, Outlander Trenton,"

Daramay said, gesturing at a widened area beside her. She, too, held a cloth.

Reluctantly, Trenton stood and moved next to her. Both women squatted beside him, one on each side, drying his feet first and working their way up to his shoulders.

Suddenly, the white stone on Marnie's forehead burst forth in a brilliant radiance. Her eyes glowed with the same light, and she froze.

Startled, Trenton looked sharply at Daramay. "What's happening to her?"

Daramay picked up the gray robe. "Hush, my outlander, Marnie is receiving a contacting, nothing more. Allow me to assist putting this on, for it is likely someone on the Circle has grown impatient."

The stone dimmed to normalcy, as did the woman's eyes. "The Circle has spoken," Marnie declared. "We are to go to the assembly hall this instant and bringing the outlander unclothed if needed."

Ignoring the robe Daramay held for the moment, Trenton strode into his suit and stepped on the pressure-sensitive latch with the front pads of his feet. The suit closed at his back and over his shoulders.

He then took the proffered gray robe from Daramay and put it on. Overlapping the front and tying it in place, he left the hood down as he moved in front of one mirror mounted on the wall.

The robe did a good job of concealing the suit, though it made him seem larger than he was. Now he looked like one of them, if there were others with brown skin and slanted almond eyes. His trimmed beard and mustache, minus the sideburns, shouldn't stand out too much. Trenton recalled a Circle member sporting something similar before Durandas had attempted to murder him.

"Shall we go, Outlander Trenton?" Daramay asked.

Marnie frowned. "Do not give him a choice to tarry. The Circle of Light is waiting."

"I suppose we must." Trenton turned his back to the mirror, suppressing a yawn. Though his head was clear, his body begged for rest.

Daramay gestured elegantly at the doorway. "Marnie shall show the way. I shall follow behind with you."

Moving quickly through the next room, they soon strode along the wide hallway, the two guards trailing behind. Daramay matched his pace, marching beside him in companionable silence.

Coming to an intersection, they crossed a hallway far larger than the earlier one, stopping at a set of guarded doors. The two white robes stationed there each had a golden sunburst emblazoned across their front, matching the one on each door. Marnie exchanged a word or two with the guards, and then they all strode into a great room inside a gigantic dome. Magnificent pillars lined a red rug luxuriously woven with many coats of arms dyed in black.

Trenton admired the expanse of the room before engaging his companion in conversation. "What need for an armed escort? Is the Circle that afraid I'm dangerous?"

Daramay glanced at him sidelong briefly. "Some of those seated on the Circle have given assurance the soldiers are for your protection."

"Except you don't really believe it, do you?"

"My beliefs are of no consequence. There are some here who may fear retaliation."

Trenton gave her a sharp look. "I'm uncertain if you contradicted me or not."

Her face smooth, Daramay kept walking. Ahead, the walkway vanished into a large pit the size of an average crater. At the edge, Marnie stopped at one side of it. Side by side, they strode by it without slowing. White marble benches lined the pit's bottom, ringed around a large smooth floor. Trent could imagine racing zip cycles around its oval circumference. A multitude of colored robes sat in the first two rows of benches.

Reaching the glass floor required a couple minutes, with most of the hooded heads following their progress. Trenton barely noticed. He concentrated instead on the twelve white and yellow robes seated behind white marble tables spaced evenly around the floor; some of those were the same people who had accosted him in the courtyard.

Daramay stopped at the last row of benches. "This is as far as I may accompany you. Please place your hands on the podium. The Circle of Light shall instruct you on the rest." The two guards had halted a row of benches behind them.

Stepping onto the circular, polished surface, Trenton strode toward a round, white marble dais, nearly losing his stride when he glanced down. The oddity he'd seen in the courtyard, the hoary, raging river of white, now churned beneath his feet. The odd substance rolled beneath the glass in turbulent glory, flowing white with bright streaks of red. Jagged red lightning flashed inside it. Trenton wrenched his eyes away. Gazing too long would make his head spin.

Trenton stepped onto the dais, going to the podium. Raised chest-high and clear as if blown from glass, the pedestal formed a toadstool that flashed with the white and red brilliance of the river below. A tube attached like a wheel around the top writhed with the same flowing matter.

Not knowing what to do next, Trenton looked around.

Durandas, the white robe who had attacked him, sat stiffly at a long table at the end of the oval. His white hair and beard provided the only recognition he needed.

Trenton thought it too bad the man wasn't close enough to lay hands upon. He'd choke the orb's location from his constricted throat somehow.

Trenton put his hands on the wheel tube.

A terrible force wrenched at Trenton's arms, pulling him away from the tube. Then the force reversed, flinging him at the pedestal hard enough to slam his hip into it. He winced.

Durandas sat suddenly within easy speaking distance, a chagrined expression on his bearded face. "I must apologize for failing to advise you about what to expect upon touching the Light Podium." His blue eyes hardened. "You are the second person to stand at the podium and claim to have arrived from another world. With the first, the truth of the matter became apparent quickly. In your case, I cannot decide. You come wearing strange garb, though different from hers, and you have something native to our world, which necessitated this special assembly. While you stand before us, you need to know the Light Podium is a way for you to personalize your plea and us to distinguish our questions. The podium will travel to whoever wishes the floor, so to speak. Do you understand?"

Trenton wondered what Durandas meant about his plea, but he merely nodded. He wanted to get this whole bloody process over. Katy was surely worried. He'd gone far too long without a status transmission. Though the zip cycle's urithium power cells would ensure it would hover beyond his lifetime, it would draw attention to his entrance into the complex. He had to get back. So many lives depended on it.

Suddenly, the Light Podium wrenched him halfway across the dome, coming to a hard stop in front of a beautiful dark-haired woman he recognized.

"Ninth Light has the podium," Durandas's voice intoned, booming throughout the dome.

Khiminay's blue eyes regarded him shortly. "You claim to have traveled here from off world, is that not so?"

"Yes."

"Where did your supposed arrival take place?"

"You know where. I arrived in your bedchamber."

Khiminay's voice boomed throughout the dome. "Let all in attendance note: there is but one exit from my chambers. Heavily warded, the barrier lay undisturbed, yet there he was!"

The dome exploded with the din of many voices shouting at once. Cries of "Dark User!" and "Infiltrator!" rang out.

Khiminay's voice rose above it, sounding triumphant. "That is not all!"

The voices cut off with a startling abruptness.

"What did you carry with you at your arrival?"

"A red orb. The orb is mine and I—"

The roars of the crowd rose again, louder this time. The stamp of many feet thundered throughout the dome with chants of "Dark User!" and "Kill him!"

Without warning, the podium wrenched him away from Khiminay as far as the room allowed. He came to an abrupt stop in front of another woman he'd met.

"Second Light has the podium," Durandas's voice intoned. The dome again fell silent.

The Lore Mother's luminous, creamy white eyes faced him from behind a large stone table constructed for someone of her towering height. "What is your plea, Outlander Trenton?"

"I have no plea, only confusion. Why attack me and take my possession?"

"This object you seek returned is the crimson orb, is it not?"

"Yes."

"What do you plan to do with the artifact? Can you interrupt the Flow? Are you a User?"

Trenton's confusion grew. "What is the Flow?"

The Lore Mother's wizened face smoothed as much as her wrinkles allowed. "What do you see when you look beneath you?"

Trenton looked down through the podium and then tore his eyes away. He gazed at the Lore Mother. "A great, frothing river of power runs beneath," he said quietly.

"Then you are a User, though you may not know it."

The voices grew loud, but the Lore Mother raised her large, wrinkled hand. The rumbles quieted. "Permit an old woman some explanation, outlander, if that is indeed what you truly are. The Circle of Light convened and summoned you before it to decide one question: are you a Dark User sent to infiltrate the White Lands' capital city? Choose your next words wisely."

Another jarring wrench brought him before a man he'd never met. His hair and beard were the light color of a sunflower, the roots darkening to a faint orange tint. The man's green eyes held a glare that fit his upturned face.

"Third Light has the podium," a voice Trenton didn't recognize intoned.

"The Lore Mother has overstepped her position. The Circle of Light shall decide what information to reveal to a potential spy," sunflower hair and beard said.

The jolt of the podium wrenched at Trenton's arm sockets almost as soon as the man's words had left his mouth.

The Lore Mother's eyes blazed brighter. "I have not relinquished the Light Podium!" Her shouted boomed throughout the dome.

Trenton's breathing beat a harsh rhythm in his ears. After climbing the tallest mountain known, recovering from a Light User attack, and then being thrown around a crater on a disc, his arms felt weak. How long did he have to hold on to the bloody thing?

The Lore Mother regarded him. At least he thought she did; it was hard to tell with her eyes the way they were. "You should know the crimson orb artifact has an affinity to Red. While we have some Red Users housed here, most are Dark Users, the sworn enemies of Light. If you claim no affiliation with them, how did you come by such a rare and powerful artifact?"

Trenton hesitated. He didn't want to blare it out to the entire assembly hall that he'd picked it up while breaking into a building. A simple, partial truth worked better than making up something. "I acquired it from a warehouse on my world of Terra."

Several voices scoffed; he heard "preposterous" more than once.

The Lore Mother's large head swiveled back and forth, her glowing white eyes shining brightly. "One more outburst from the hall and the Circle shall install a sound barrier."

The hall quieted.

Satisfied, the Lore Mother continued. "Though far from certain, the most common belief conjectures the crimson orb has some ability to function as a travel gateway. Is this how you arrived?"

Trenton thought about it. The orb wasn't the only thing in the room. "No. I believe sapphire obelisks brought me here."

The hall exploded with cries and loud conversation.

Then silence closed in with such abruptness, he wondered if he'd suddenly gone deaf.

Two members of the Circle of Light's right hands glowed white, a clear tube stretched to the frothing river below. A translucent dome now covered the Circle with him in the middle, perhaps the sound barrier the Lore Mother had spoken of.

"This revelation changes all," the Lore Mother declared loudly. "I call for a counting. The artifact must return to the outlander!" A bright white ring lit up on the Light Podium's wheel. "My circle is cast," the old woman added.

The light podium flitted smoothly. This time to the next on the Circle, a woman with brown hair and hard eyes. Though she said nothing, a second white circle lit up beside the Lore Mother's circle, and then he was off to a jovial-faced man next in the circle from her.

Trenton faced Durandas last. Seven white circles ringed the podium with four black ones. One of the black, Khiminay's, had surprised and disappointed him.

Durandas regarded Trenton for many heartbeats. Then, his lips tightened and once again Trenton stood in the center of the floor.

The Flow drained from the Light Podium and only the hollow, glass-like tube remained. "I, Durandas, First Light of the Circle of Light, invoke the right to delay the counting for one full day. This matter is too critical to take the outlander at his word; additional research is necessary. The Circle of Light shall reconvene at this bell tomorrow."

Durandas's soft but firm voice rang through Trenton's mind with the harshness of a howling wind. He blinked rapidly while quashing the urge to yell at the bloody Circle about the unfairness of the declaration. But it would do no good. The First Light had decided. Some of those in the Circle didn't like it. They cast dark looks at his retreating back as the white-robed man climbed the stairs two at a time leading out of the pit, but they would all do as he'd decreed.

Trenton stepped from the dais, meeting the Lore Mother and Daramay in the center. "What now?" he asked, not caring who answered.

The Lore Mother spoke. "Daramay shall show you to your room. Relax and continue to heal. The First Light shall have no choice but to return the artifact to your possession tomorrow, though you will not have the freedom to leave until we have studied it along with how you use it. Durandas cannot invoke the right to delay twice on the same matter, though he exercised the maximum time allowed."

The Lore Mother's words instilled questions and concerns.

"I can't leave anyway unless you have a gateway. Do you have one? I have to return to my world and soon, or many may die. What will Durandas do with the orb for a full day? Will he convince enough of the others to change the counting in his favor?" Trenton asked in a rush.

"Alas, there is no off-world gateway here," the Lore Mother said, her raspy voice soft. "Durandas may change some minds in the time he has allotted. The counting was close. Though most on the Circle will not budge once they have cast, and he has raised the ire of more than a few by invoking the right of delay. The Circle does not like to have its decisions suspended. This is strange... the First Light has never exercised this tactic in the past, so I do not know what to think of it." The Lore Mother turned to Daramay. "Make certain to treat him as a guest. See that you meet his primary needs before you retire."

"Yes, Mother," Daramay said, inclining her head slightly.

The Lore Mother turned the direction the First Light had gone. "Now, I shall go pummel some sense into that fool Durandas. I cannot think what has come over him. I bid you both good night."

Daramay gestured at the opposite staircase. "Please, walk with me, Trenton. Let us go to your quarters."

"Gladly," Trenton said. He'd had enough of the flitting Light Podium and the bloody Circle of Light for one day. Thanks in a large part because of the blasted First Light. As they climbed from the pit, he wondered if he was going to have to find a way to kill the man.

Chapter Five
The Flow

THE DOOR TO THE First Light's quarters was silver, and solid from the look of it. Not quite what Trenton would've expected from someone as high and mighty as Durandas.

"I'm surprised the First Light settled for a silver door. We've passed other doors made from gold," Trenton said casually, though softly. Even at this early bell, he had little certainty the hall would remain as deserted as his guide believed it would.

Daramay cast a quick glance his way and lowered her head demurely. His heart raced from her simple action. They'd sat up quietly speaking for most of the night, and her practice of lowering her head shyly and then looking up boldly through her bangs at him was endearing. Of no surprise, the talking had led to cuddling. Convincing her to bring him here had taken little requesting afterward.

Staring up at him, her wide blue eyes blinking slowly through her bangs, Daramay replied, her voice hushed. "I am uncertain of your meaning. Mere gold would not do for the most high on the Circle. Silver has signified the office of the First Light from the beginning. I have heard Durandas attempted to have it changed early in his appointment. He wanted a wooden door installed, and this one melted down for the Circle's coffers. The Circle of Light at that time threatened to ask for his resignation for demanding it."

Trenton almost wished they had asked for his departure. Perhaps then he wouldn't have the situation he had now, stuck on a planet with no way to return without the crystal orb while his people died in his home world. After mulling it over, he was certain it had activated the obelisks. However, he wasn't about to tell a soul here that. Not even Daramay. Convincing her he intended to prove to Durandas he came from another world hadn't been that hard. She seemed to want to believe him.

Now if he could just convince the First Light. Trenton hoped showing the man what his climate-control suit was capable of would be enough to get him to change his opinion. Then perhaps he would give the orb back and even help him activate a gateway if he could locate one. Daramay didn't know of any.

Daramay paused with her hand on the door. "Strange," she said.

"What is it?"

"There is no ward on his door. A Circle member's entry always has one. We keep acolytes whose sole duty it is to verify the Circle members have set a nightly ward. This is a high honor."

"So, it's there for protection?"

"Yes, and also a deterrent. Someone stronger with the Flow than Durandas would have to break it. Even then, he would know the instant it happened..." Her last words grew soft as the door swung slowly open from her gentle push.

"I don't suppose it should've had a mechanical lock also?"

"The First Light would have ensured it remained locked personally."

Trenton slipped past her into the room. "Stay behind me then. Something's wrong."

The chairs and small gilded tables of the greeting room all appeared intact, but things in the next room were in chaos. Broken, overturned tables and chairs lay about, and shattered glass and porcelain fragments speckled the place. The rugs and walls had scorch marks on them, while dust and crumbled porcelain décor lay wherever he looked. The acrid smell of smoke filled the air.

"The First Light!" Daramay yelled. Charging past him, she vanished through the splintered frame of a doorway.

"Wait!" he shouted, knowing she wouldn't. Trenton sprinted after Daramay. Dashing through the ransacked quarters, he found her unmoving in the main bedchamber, her beautiful face scrunched in fear.

Daramay stared at an enormous blue marble bed cleaved in half by something powerful enough to break the hard stone. A dark bloodstain splattered the white sheets.

Trenton put his arms around her, looking beyond the destruction. The far wall had scorch marks at regular intervals leading away to the right.

Releasing Daramay, Trenton moved to that side of the bed. As he suspected, a small pool of blood lay at the base of the split, the marble chipped and pitted on both sides of the gaping crack. Blood splatters left a trail leading to another room. Trenton followed. Inside, a small stream of water pooled at a natural basin before vanishing under a rock wall, though he barely noticed. At the back, a pair of topaz crystal obelisks stood. A thrill of hope surged through him.

Glancing back, Trenton made certain Daramay remained where he'd left her, and then he walked around the pool, checking the floor carefully. One fingertip-sized drop of blood lay at the base of the gateway. When nothing else of interest presented itself in the room, he made his way back to the bedchamber.

"What happened to him? Is he in there?" Daramay asked softly as soon as she came near, her eyes wide with fright.

"No he's not, but there is something else."

Daramay's blue eyes grew rounder. She looked beyond frightened. Trenton wanted to take her in his arms and promise her he would protect her, always.

"What is it? Is it someone else? I know I'm supposed to handle it. I'm a healer, but I don't like death. I never have. Please don't tell anyone."

Trenton slipped his arms around her then and gave her a quick, fierce squeeze. Pulling back, he clasped her hand. "Come with me."

Daramay allowed him to lead her through the door and around the pool. She gasped when she noticed the obelisks.

"Can you activate them?" he asked, smiled.

Daramay looked at him with sadness, shaking her head. "I cannot."

Trenton's smile faded, his excitement draining faster than the pool in the room. "Then it's over. Without the orb, I cannot go home."

"No, it is not over, not completely. You can... You might..." Daramay whispered.

Trenton stared. "I don't understand."

"You do not have to go. Stay here with me. You know this, yet you will not." Glistening with building tears, the deep blue pools of her eyes pleaded with him to disagree.

He could not.

When no answer came after a time, her eyes leaked her disappointment. Daramay looked away at the floor. "Can you see the Flow?" she asked, her voice cracking slightly with the last word.

"What?"

"Can you see the river of power flowing beneath your feet?"

Trenton looked down. The great, stormy river was there, waiting for him. "Yes," he said softly.

"Listen and follow everything I say completely. With the lightest touch imaginable, brush against the Flow with a thought, draw the tiniest bit in through your hand, then sever the connection."

Trenton reached out to the river, to the Flow. Brilliant red hues raged past, crackling with unimaginable power. He created a link to a single strand. Energy filled him. Power. Suddenly, for the first time in his life, he was alive.

Daramay's shout rang out, echoing as if from the bottom of a deep pit. "Now send it into the center of the obelisks, all of it!"

Power flowed inside him, sweet and divine. With it, he had the strength to accomplish the things he'd long desired. With it, he had a way to remove the king and his administration. He would be king. With it, he had the power to wave away the radiation and save Terra, to save his friends. How could he let it go? Why would he ever let it go?

Daramay's voice echoed in his mind from a long distance, a small intrusion upon his thoughts. "Sever the connection! Please,

Trenton! You are still drawing it in, too much! Release the Flow now!"

Daramay was right. He had to use his precious Flow to open the gateway, to find the red orb if he wanted it back. Did he need it now that he had unlimited power? No, that's not true, he thought. There was a limit to the reservoir of his body, a depth he couldn't surpass or he would overflow. He'd nearly reached it. The wellspring filling the vessel that was him would soon overflow. Once it did, Trenton sensed he'd not be able to stop the Flow pouring in. The power would consume him.

Trenton severed the connection and raised his hand, sending the entire pool of power hurtling between the topaz obelisks as a red-flamed comet. Striking an unseen barrier, the red flames spread upon impact and rippled through a curtain of darkness. A gateway spiraled between the obelisks, raging in a constant flux.

Trenton could still sense the Flow, succulent and sweet. Now that he'd accessed it, it would always seem within reach, but he was wary of drawing upon it again. The Flow streamed in its rawest form. The mindlessness of such power could—no, would—vaporize anyone or anything foolish enough to stand in its path, accidental or otherwise.

Yet he longed for it.

He'd found his limit with the Flow; the red orb would increase it. Trenton now understood why the First Light hadn't wanted to give it back.

Trenton focused on Daramay. Her lovely eyes were frightened, filled with fear of his leaving. He wanted to remain with her always. He felt so alive. Now that he had the Flow, he could accomplish much here. He could stay with her.

He had to have the orb.

"Come with me, Daramay. We'll find Durandas together." Trenton reached for her hand. "He's hurt and may need your healing."

Moving her arms behind her, Daramay shook her head softly from side to side. "My place is here, helping those of Surbo. We are a city at war. The wounded come every day, broken and bleeding, from defending the crumbling walls. My use of the Flow heals many; the need for one like me is great. Would you give up the orb and remain by my side? You are a User, a strong User. Your magic could aid me greatly and help us. The entire city. Few have the strength to open a gateway. You shall have high status here."

Trenton found it hard to believe she thought him strong; he didn't think so. Not yet, but there is a way, he thought. He'd felt it with the orb. "I have to follow Durandas. Something happened here."

Daramay's beautiful face drooped with sorrow briefly, then firmed, her lips compressing to a thin line. "So, you would decide to leave me then. Wait a little, I shall return quickly." She dashed out of the room.

Trenton barely had time to wonder about Daramay's sudden departure before she returned. "Take these. You shall need them." Daramay handed him a thick-hafted silver dagger in a sheath and an amber crystal disc. "The dagger will supply you with much coin if you have it melted down. The glimmer shard disc is flawless. Find a master infuser to infuse it with light as soon as you have coin. The shard will light your way, so you needn't drain yourself simply to illuminate your path."

Though he didn't understand fully what she meant, Trenton pulled open the gray robe and took the offered items from her shaking hands. He put the disc in a pocket and clipped the dagger to his hip. Retying the gray robe, he wrapped Daramay in his arms and kissed her. Her lips were soft yet firm. He tasted her sweetness mingled with the salt of her tears. His body stirred from her heady scent. He wanted to know her completely, but the orb tugged at his thoughts. He pulled back, breathless from the kiss.

Daramay hugged him tightly, her breath also coming in gasps. "The gateway shall close behind you. I could not follow if I so desired. If you are to return for me, it is upon you alone."

When he stood back and faced the gate, Daramay released him without resistance. Trenton took one last look at her round eyes of blue and then stepped through.

CHAPTER SIX

BEYOND TERRA

THE TOPAZ OBELISKS DEPOSITED Trenton inside a granite structure with a brown marble floor, flecked with gray and worn smooth from the tread of many feet. He searched for traces of blood. Nothing obvious caught his eye, though he could easily miss small drops. When he looked behind him, the solid, empty wall made him think of Daramay. A pang of loss stabbed him.

The small alcove Trenton stood in overlooked a grand rectangular open space a story below. A wide stair brought him to the main floor, where great pillars supported an arched roof. Colored tiles, painted with an expert hand, formed fields, mountains, ponds, and lakes brushed with fine strokes. Trenton would have liked to take his time gazing at the lush painted greenery, but the magnificent gateway built into the end wall two stories high drew his attention.

People waited to pass manned checkpoints to use the gateway as armed soldiers stood vigilant on both sides. A single, wide strip left clear for new arrivals allowed travelers to pass by the podiums unimpeded.

Moving away from the openness of the steps, Trenton found a bench and sat down to watch the operation, wondering what the clerks required to pass. The answer came after a short while. Each person presented a marker, which the clerks at the podiums collected.

The probability that Durandas had gone that way was unlikely. The First Light would've had to have the marker on him before his attack, and the likelihood he could've grabbed it as he made his escape was low. Trenton ruled the gateway out, which left everywhere else to search.

Sighing, Trenton stood, striding without haste in the opposite direction toward a high spanning archway providing an opening outside. A woman holding a blue and white parasol and wearing a sheer blue dress sat demurely on a bench beside it. Her hair was a darker gold than Daramay's.

The woman rose gracefully as Trenton neared. Striding easily on high-heeled boots, she matched his pace, her eyes searching his. "I am Corteezsha. I greet you, traveler. Where do you hail from?" Corteezsha's long black eyelashes fluttered above her russet eyes. Trenton longed for Daramay's blue ones.

Beyond the archway, tall, robed and armored statues kept a stern eye on those bold enough to pass below. Male or female, the carved faces displayed no mirth. The statues seemed to portray his feelings on companionship. The few he desired to have around him were now lost: one back at Surbo, and many on Terra.

"I have made it my mission to show you around Gray Dust. I must say, your arrival was unorthodox. Having just left from there, I know that the alcove you stepped down from was empty." Corteezsha gave him a gauging look.

"I must apologize if I seem brusque, my lady, but I have little need for an escort. I desire my privacy, if you will."

"I..." A protest dying on her lips, Corteezsha slowed and then stopped.

Trenton kept going, striding along the walkway between the gigantic statues of men and women garbed in their robes or armor, their blank stone eyes somehow judging. Going by their expressions, they found him lacking.

The end of the cobblestone pathway heralded a large city of architectural brown stone and wood. He paused at the last of the statues' bases, looking off into the distance. The vaporous dust of loose dirt and sand pervading the air brought stark memories of the radiation haze of Low Realm. He could lose his bearings in a metropolis that size without even knowing he had—something to avoid at all costs.

A quick glance behind showed him the woman had continued toward him. Perhaps he'd been too hasty to turn down her offer to guide him. Trenton waited, staring upon the city spread inside a great oasis surrounded by the desolation of a deadly desert. As naïve as a child, he'd opened a gateway to this world of magic and violence beyond Terra. Now he had to find the red orb and use it to return home. Too many lives depended upon it. The pragmatic part of him knew he would need help with such an enormous, perhaps impossible, task.

Corteezsha halted as close beside him as the blue and white parasol allowed. "As a flourishing patch of greenery at the threshold of Great Dune, Gray Dust is impressive, is it not?"

"Yes, it sprawls for some distance, seemingly with little planning, which makes my task quite daunting."

"Might I inquire about your task? Perhaps I shall have the resources to lighten the heaviness in your voice when you speak of it, sire."

Trenton regarded her. Slowly twirling her parasol, she looked down at the city with a proud, half-smile locked on her full, red lips. Corteezsha seemed sincere, and he needed a guide. "Call me Trenton. I hunt for a man. A specific one."

Corteezsha tinkled with laughter, like fine titanium wind chimes caught in a playful breeze. "Why, Trenton, surely you jest. Most unspoken-for women, like myself, hunt for the right man. Few men here do."

"This man has something of great importance to me."

Corteezsha smiled. "Then I believe I shall be of much help. Hunting a man has been a particular interest of mine for quite some time. Though I daresay over half the women in Gray Dust would make a similar claim."

"This man is prominent in the Circle of Light."

Corteezsha's smile faded. "Whatever would a Circle of Light User have that would merit hunting him? You play at a deadly game. The Circle's Users are some of the most powerful in all the White Lands. Perhaps you are much more dangerous a man than I first believed."

"You will not help me then?"

Corteezsha's beautiful face grew less solemn. Her russet eyes had a mischievous glint. "I have not yet denied you. You fascinate me. Come with me to my sources. Someone will have heard of your quarry."

"Vermin, such as her and her sources, will make you the prey," someone behind them said.

Trenton spun.

A woman wearing a red shawl strode toward them. Someone he'd met.

Khiminay paused a short distance away, regarding Corteezsha with cold interest. "By now this woman has made you the mark, and those shadowy figures lurking beyond the statues wait for the signal to move in for the kill. Or capture, depending on her motives."

Trenton took a step away from Corteezsha, glancing at the row of statues on each side as he did. Khiminay was right. At least two forms loitered at the third and fourth statues.

"What are you after?" Trenton demanded of Corteezsha, disappointed with himself. He felt foolish for trusting her as much as he had.

The wide-eyed surprise on Corteezsha's face vanished quickly. Standing relaxed, she twirled her parasol nonchalantly. A light blue, translucent glow suddenly enveloped her. Had he not been staring at her, he would've thought it a mirage of the dry, hot air. "I told you. I simply want to assist you with your search. Is this woman known to you?" With a flourish, she closed the parasol.

Trenton fired his cutter, stepped behind her, and reached over her shoulder to put her in a headlock, but something repelled him... the azure barrier.

Twisting to the side and flashing him her widest smile, Corteezsha ran past him toward the city. Trenton let her go.

Khiminay's right hand glowed faintly red as several men came out from behind the statues, moving toward them quickly. One, a tall bare-chested man, carried a large, long-hafted hammer slung over a shoulder. No match for his long stride, the big man pulled ahead of the others, only to have a fireball smash into his chest, covering him in flames. His shape outlined in orange briefly, larger than normal. He kept coming, the flames blowing away at the speed of his charge.

The others had no such protection. In rapid succession, the three men in the lead behind the giant fell burning, and then the man was upon Trenton, drawing his sole attention. The mighty hammer swung with frightening speed aimed for his head even as the big man skidded to a halt.

Stooping under the blow, Trenton shuffled away, gaining distance between himself and his assailant. The hammer reversed, the man whipping it at him with a backswing executed in mid-swing. Trenton rocked back on the balls of his feet. The gust of wind from the narrow miss billowed into his face, blowing a stray lock of hair into his eye. Trenton shook it out of his vision quickly. Obviously an expert fighter, the man wouldn't hesitate to use any sign of weakness to his advantage.

Huge hammer held at the ready, the big man circled him, seeking an opening.

Presenting a smaller target, Trenton turned to one side, slipped the silver dagger from its sheath, and powered the cutter. Tracking the man's movements, he rotated with him, staying just out of range of the hammer. As they revolved, he got a quick glimpse of Khiminay, her arm with the glowing hand extended away from him. He was on his own, which was fine with him; it seemed he had always been. Trenton waited for the man to signal his next move. There was always some small sign.

Trenton caught sight of what he was looking for a moment later as a small intake of breath and a subtle shift of the left knee.

Trenton stepped in and pushed the hammer thrust away from his chest with the dagger, letting it glance off his right shoulder. He raked downward with the cutter. Nearly half the hammer dropped to the ground, neatly severed. With his heel, Trenton dragged the weapon behind him by its wide head.

The big man grunted. Raising the bar of steel as a club, he hesitated, his brown eyes cautious. Jumping backward, he turned and ran the same way Corteezsha had.

Sheathing the dagger and severing the cutter's power, Trenton picked up the half-hammer while monitoring the rest of the assailants.

Khiminay sent two red missiles streaking toward four men who ran for the shelter of the stone building. "That is the last of them," she said casually. Her missiles slammed into the wall beside the first man through the door. Dust billowed outward. "I thought it best to ensure they kept going. They would still have us outnumbered four to one should they convince the four who crept away first to attempt another charge."

"A wise send-off."

Khiminay laughed, her amusement making him smiled. Then he, too, laughed, feeling the tenseness of the battle drop away. His right shoulder throbbed dully

Khiminay's face smoothed as she appraised him. "You fight well for an outlander."

"What did they want with me?"

"There are many reasons for such scum to want a healthy male specimen like you. Forced servitude is the most common, either as a mercenary guard or as courtesan services for the wealthy elites in this city, both men and women."

The pit of his stomach weakened with nausea. Without her timely arrival, his capture would've been imminent. "I owe you much for this. You fight well for an Off-worlder."

Khiminay smiled.

Trenton flashed a brief smile back. "I suppose we should get moving. Someone is bound to come out of that gateway structure."

"Yes. Likely the city watch already has had a contacting, alerted by someone inside of the fighting out here. There are those who indenture in the coliseum with the ability to communicate in that way. There is little time left to us and I must complete the task I risked traveling here to perform." Reaching into the bosom of her green dress, Khiminay held out the crimson orb.

Trenton gaped.

"Take it before I cannot relinquish it."

Wondering what she meant, Trenton slipped it from her hand. As soon as he touched it, he thought of only it. The orb remembered his touch; it knew him. An immense sense of satisfaction filled him to the core, a wondrous feeling of completeness. An audible click echoed through his equilibrium, swaying him on his feet.

"Are you well?"

Trenton struggled through the orb's joy to form words. "I don't understand. How did you come by my orb? Durandas wounded—"

"Durandas, set it all up," Khiminay said briskly. "The First gained blood from a butcher and cast about his chambers with the Flow breaking his own furniture. I suspect someone on the council may have helped."

"Daramay! Is she all right?"

"Yes, she played her part well. I found her leaving Durandas's chambers. The healer insisted you had broken into the First Light's chambers, stolen the orb, and left wounded through the topaz gateway. However, there was a flaw in her story, a big one. Such an act would require someone powerful in the Flow to dissolve the ward placed by the First Light on his doorway. Even I cannot accomplish it. However, with the seal broken, or not installed in the first place, I could search the chambers. Discovering the hiding place of the crystal orb did not take long. The Flow revealed it inside an illusion stone, tucked away in the room with the topaz gate."

Trenton heard her words, but his mind grappled with the first few. Daramay worked with the First Light. He put a hand to his stomach as another bout of nausea struck.

"Did the colossal man wound you?"

"I don't believe so. The hammer's blow was only a glancing one to my shoulder."

Khiminay frowned. "Show me. Make haste, we have little time."

Trenton untied his gray robe and pulled it back, exposing his right shoulder. Two of the suit's magnetic links had bent a little, though it had done its job of absorbing most of the damage. Such a minor blow had caused much destruction, though all the links had the benefit of vitanium. Even the cutter couldn't burn through one.

Khiminay touched the spot with her delicate fingers. "Oddly, I have no sense of an infusion spreading. The hammer had the radiance leak of a master infusion until you severed it. How did you accomplish that?"

Then she paused, her light blue eyes searching around. "Don't answer that. We shall save it for the next time we meet. Go now, follow the cobble road a short way to the city. Look for the Quench Quarters Inn and Tavern across the intersection there. Here, take this." She pressed a small leather bag into his hand. "Pay for two weeks' lodging, one week at a time. I shall meet you there as soon as the Circle has calmed."

Khiminay paused again, moving close.

Trenton gazed into her eyes. Red pulses moved across her corneas from left to right in a mesmerizing line.

Khiminay kissed him then, long and passionate. "Go," she said huskily, turning away. "I shall delay the Circle as long as I can if they should come through before I gate back to Surbo."

Breathless, Trenton watched her leave for a few beats of his racing heart, his mind whirling. When had Khiminay decided she cared for him?

Trenton willed his legs into motion and headed the direction Khiminay had mentioned. Stone buildings—some brown, others white—loomed at the end of an old cobblestone road wide enough for two wagons to pass.

Trenton thought about Daramay as he walked, his anger growing and mixing with the hated emotion of betrayal. He'd trusted her. Leaving Daramay had come harder than he'd wanted to admit. Knowing now she'd duped him from the first made him feel foolish to believe he could count on his own judgment. How could he trust himself with anyone here?

One thing he knew was that staying alive meant blending in on Astura. The best way to accomplish it was to befriend a native. Befriend, but not trust.

This world beyond Terra had proven incapable of instilling confidence. Everywhere he went here was cutthroat, something he'd have to adapt to, and quickly.

Chapter Seven

Awareness

Trenton was halfway down a gentle incline heading to the city when soldiers entered from an intersection and began to march toward him. Pulling the hood of his robe over his head, he left the road and slipped beside a brown granite or limestone building—it was hard to tell with all the dust on it—and pressed himself against the wall in the shadows. The armored patrol hurried by, marching past at a fair clip.

As soon as he judged it safe, Trenton strode onto the road at a relaxed pace, extending the distance between him and the patrol without being obvious...he hoped.

The tavern was located where Khiminay described it, on the far side of an intersection. It was built to last with big blocks of tan granite. Mounted to the underside of a wide awning, a masterfully painted sign depicted a lithe woman wearing sheer lace.

The woman was in the act of pulling a string tied to the stopper of a cask of ale hung above her wide, lifelike green eyes and flowing brown hair. The words, "Quench Quarters Inn and Tavern," daubed boldly above the image made him aware he'd found the right place.

Chafing at the delay, Trenton allowed an assortment of horse- and ox-drawn wagons, small camel-powered caravans led by swarthy men wearing gaudy colors of silks, and armored men and women carrying weaponry to pass. Finally, he weaved a path across the intersection, keeping his distance whenever possible from leather-vested men and women sporting sheathed swords, axes, hammers, long knives, and even bows and crossbows.

Trenton marveled at the variety even as he grew uneasy with each sighting. Astura was obviously a world where fighting was commonplace.

A weathered mahogany chair propped open the front door of the tavern, inviting him to enter the dusky interior.

Even at midday, the Quench Quarters had only a few tables left unoccupied. A solemn-faced man worked at filling two trays of tankards as two tavern maidens chatted quietly with each other at the end of a long bar. Trenton caught the man's eye by resting his elbows on the bar and leaning forward. "I seek lodging," he said simply.

The man grunted. "My wife, Sabella, handles that." He nodded toward a tall woman surveying the room with a hawkish eye from a doorway at the rear.

Sabella singled him out as he stepped away from the bar. Trenton strode to her.

"You looking to room with us?" she asked, the tone of her voice as solemn as the man's face. The woman was trim and fit though aged to the latter part of her middle seasons. A white lock streaked her blonde hair, but her face was smooth of most lines. Her low-cut black dress, ending at mid-thigh, matched the attire of the tavern maidens.

"Yes."

Sabella regarded him closely, her gray eyes penetrating. "How long have you planned to stay? The cost is slightly less for extended lodging. Do you wish a regular room or deluxe? Deluxe has two meals a day included and a heated bath."

Trenton recalled the heavy bag Khiminay had pressed into his palm, the one he still carried that way. His fist closed about it. "The deluxe room, if you please."

The corner of Sabella's mouth tugged upward slightly, and her shoulders relaxed a little.

Trenton hesitated with the length of the stay. Khiminay had mentioned a week or possibly two. He didn't have a week, perhaps only a day; things were desperate by now back on Terra. Yet what did it matter? The bag Khiminay had given him was her coffers. If Khiminay wanted to fund a week, then he would purchase one.

"For one week, perhaps two after the first," he said.

"A bronze rectangle per week will cover the cost, half up front."

Trenton opened the bag. Only gold and silver were visible. Hoping it was enough, he slipped a golden square out and dropped it into her palm.

The coin vanished into her bosom. Sabella smiled. "That will do nicely for both weeks. Tonight's first ale is on the house with your supper in half a bell. After, one of my tavern maidens will show you to your room. Should you desire her companionship for additional coin, simply tell her or let her know you wish to peruse someone else. The Quench Quarters have many to choose from, human or nonhuman."

Surprised by the woman's bold words, Trenton wondered what the innkeeper meant by nonhuman, but he had to stay focused. "How does one get a mark to use the topaz gate?"

Sabella's gray eyes glittered, pulsing with minute flecks of violet he hadn't noticed before. The woman was a mystery, and still lovely at her age. "The hooded man has controlled the ascension gateway in Old Town Coliseum for half my life. He owes no favors to anyone, though he may provide a mark to one such as I with the right form of payment... provided from each of us. I will inquire if you are good to me."

Trenton paused. Coupled with the bartender and half again his seasons, surely Sabella wasn't flirting with him. Perhaps she means his coins. "Speak your price."

Glancing toward the bar, Sabella smiled briefly. "Do not be too quick to part with your coin; we both come at a steep cost. What is the reason for your travel? The hooded man will ask."

"I have business there."

Sabella laughed. "That is the standard answer and rarely works. When you have a better one, send a maiden for me. I will come to your room and discuss it... at length. Please choose a table while I ensure you receive proper attention."

Glad to escape her predatory gaze, Trenton turned to the room already filling with patrons behind him. He needed to know more about the gate and the man running it. Buying someone tankards of ale may prove fruitful.

In a dimly lit corner, an elegant woman and a little girl with stark white skin sat at a large table with a broad-shouldered older warrior wearing an eye patch that partially covered a large scar. The sleek creature sitting on the floor beside the woman made him gawk. Sienna fur covered a feline-like body and wolfish head, much larger than the extinct wolves on Terra. The creature's amber hourglass eyes regarded his every step as he crossed the room and stopped at the table.

With a slender finger, the woman brushed a stray lock of auburn hair from hard aqua eyes that stared at him with distrust. "What do you want?"

"A trade, if you will. A large pitcher of the finest ale that is available in this wonderful establishment for simple information."

The grizzled warrior thumped his mug on the table, his hand going to rest on of one of the axes that hung on each of his hips. His one blue eye fixed upon Trenton though he spoke to those sitting at the table. "I cannot vouch for him, since I don't know him personally. I say send him on his way."

The little girl's green eyes stared at him blankly, standing out starkly upon her disturbingly pale skin and dark black hair. "He has not been long on this world," she said. Her voice had an odd echoing quality to it, as if coming from a great distance.

The man and the woman glanced sharply at her, and even the creature's noble head tilted toward the strange little girl.

Trenton didn't bother to hide his surprise. Was he so obviously an Outlander? "Will you allow me to provide some dinner, then? I'm a traveler only just arrived, as your young companion has made known. I require knowledge of travel gateways."

The woman exchanged an abrupt look with the girl, whose eyes now seemed the normal, lively eyes of someone nine or ten seasons. The little girl gave a little girl shrug.

Then, oddly, the woman turned to the creature sitting on its haunches beside her, who inclined its wolf's head slightly.

"I say let him move on. Nothing he's said has changed my mind," the warrior spat when she gazed at him last, one fine eye-brow raised.

The woman turned to him; her intriguing blue eyes as hard as plasicrete. "You'd bet-ter sit down and get that food on its way. We're famished. Two of our companions are attending the horses. Order for them too, if you will. After we eat, we'll talk about how gateways are difficult to come by and what you want with one."

Trenton beckoned to a tavern maiden car-rying a tray of filled mugs two tables away. A man wearing black plate armor, though only one gauntlet covered his left hand, tried to get her attention with a light touch on her shoulder with his bared right. She stiffened from the touch, but kept her eyes upon Trenton.

Satisfied he had caught the maiden's at-tention, Trenton once again stared at the elegant woman's solemn face. It was the most beautiful he'd ever seen. Something had embittered her deeply, razing her to the core. Suddenly he wanted to see her smile, to know she was capable of it.

The orb's comforting presence bulged in the right leg pocket of his suit as he sat. Questions scrolled through his mind. Why had Durandas defied the Circle and worked on an elaborate ruse to steal it? Khiminay had risked a lot to give it back, though she was a User and could have kept it for her personal use. Why had she traveled far to find and then return it to him? What game were they playing?

The elegant woman gestured to the one-eyed warrior. "This is Hastel, our self-imposed guardian. The girl is Atoi, and beside her is our warden companion. His name pronunciation is too long for human lips. Call him Broth. You should know who you are about to dine with. I am Crystalyn, Crystalyn Creek. Do you still want to remain at our table?"

"Why wouldn't I? I'm Trenton Bonner," he replied, glancing behind him for the serving maiden. What's taking so long?

Her steps coming in abrupt jerks, the maiden was nearly to their table, drenched from the empty drink tray she carried.

Trenton frowned at the maiden. "Hey, you're spilling it!"

Broth growled.

Atoi's weird voice echoed through Trenton, and her eyes had dulled again. "It comes, Vessel of Ages."

Hastel fumbled for an axe. "Blast it! What comes?"

A green symbol, beautiful with its many spinning cones inside, similar to the radiation funnel clouds that sometimes hit the Wasted Sea on Low Realm, hovered in front of Crystalyn, but not for long. The symbol streaked across the table to him, unraveling as it came.

A concussive gust of wind struck Trenton and flung him backward across the room, sucking the breath from him as it pressed him to the floor, roaring past at an incredible rate.

Finally, the gale slowed, losing its roar to the constant drone of a slowly fading breeze. The serving maiden lay beside him. Hit with the brunt of the symbol, the woman was out cold, or dead. Trenton reached for her, searching for a pulse.

"Don't touch her. There is something going on here. I suspect a flicker is involved." Crystalyn said, her voice slightly higher than normal.

Trenton froze. He pulled his hand back. He did not know what she meant, but it didn't sound good.

The maiden's hand reached out and grabbed his.

An awareness stabbed into Trenton's mind. Dark and resolute, it swallowed his frontal lobe, his sense of himself in great chunks, overwriting who he was with something alien, something immensely powerful. Part of him recoiled in a corner, desperately wanting to hide.

There was nowhere to go.

The darkness loomed immense, crowding into his mind. The last of him shrank, compressed small, shrinking tiny. Malice, supreme in the knowledge of absolute subversion, bore down upon him. A great intelligence, conjoined with many others, resonated with anticipation.

Something golden pierced the darkness between him and the malice: a symbol, a symbol with the feel of an elegant woman. Her awareness was confident, though wary, and too late.

Blackness engulfed him.

CHAPTER EIGHT

THE PRICE

SOMETHING BROWN FADED INTO clarity. A partially sloped ceiling. Sparse details emerged. Roughhewn wooden trusses stained brown. A tiny girl's small head covered with jet-black hair leaning over him, a flicker of interest apparent from her wide, emerald eyes. Did he know her?

The girl's oddly pale brow furrowed. "He's stirring. You said he was going to stand before Onan, but he awakes."

A head full of auburn hair joined the girl on his other side. Blue eyes of ice peered at him, angry eyes.

"I said it was likely he would meet the Great Father, Atoi. He appears to have decided to remain with the living for a while longer, though I cannot say if his neural processes survived fully."

Her pale face smoothing, Atoi withdrew.

A shockingly gigantic, though beautiful, woman's head replaced the girl's tiny one. Her glowing white eyes were as bright as the Lore Mother's eyes were back in Surbo. Her flowing hair curled past her shoulders. "Can he speak?" Pleasant and melodious, the large woman's voice was a pleasant surprise.

Crystalyn's hard eyes softened slightly. "Can you?"

With a start, Trenton realized he couldn't feel anything below his neck. Had he lost more than my legs this time? Panic grew. Opening his mouth to ask, he emitted only a guttural grunt.

Crystalyn looked across him at the big woman. "There you have it, Lore Rayna. He cannot answer your inquiries, at least for now. I imagine he cannot even move, though the paralysis should pass."

Crystalyn's words relieved some of his fear.

Lore Rayna sat back, raising her knees. Even sitting on the floor, she was nearly level with Crystalyn standing. "As far as we are aware, only your sister Jade and I survived a similar psychic attack. Now he makes three. Are you certain the tavern maiden had no mind worm infection?"

"Positive. My gut instinct says something different pursues us. This makes the second similar evil I grappled with after cleaning it from Jade in the Vale. The attack in Brown Recluse had the strongest power. I nearly succumbed to that one."

Lore Rayna stood, towering over Crystalyn. Her leafy green dress adjusted of its own accord to cover her upper thighs. "As my mistress believes, so shall I." Moving with an agility surprising for one her size, the big woman left Trenton's view, taking the living dress with her.

Everything seemed so surreal. In a real way, this world had larger problems than Terra.

Crystalyn eyed him. "When you can speak, we will talk. I would like to know how you have in your possession an artifact I'm familiar with." Reaching into her dress pocket, she pulled out the red crystal orb. Flashing it briefly in front of his eyes, her hands moved lower, beyond his vision. "I have put it back in your pocket."

Crystalyn's beautiful but solemn face grew sterner, as if she packed the demands of every living thing that breathed on this world around with her. "Know this, Trenton. I will have the truth from you or I'll take it from you using less pleasant methods. I have the capability and the determination. Complete honesty is necessary. There are many lives I hold dearly at stake, one of them my own."

Trenton tried to assure her he would, but nothing came out.

A thump resounded from the direction of the door, followed by two others.

"Should I let her in this time, mistress?" the warrior, Hastel, inquired from somewhere nearby, his voice raspy.

"I suppose you must."

A small creak of floorboards preceded a woman Trenton recalled.

Sabella, shorter and more robust than Crystalyn, came into view opposite Crystalyn. "He's awake."

Seen from below, Sabella's low-cut blouse seemed lower than before. Sabella flashed him a coy smile and then looked at Crystalyn. "You should rest now, my lady. You're nearly as pale as your little companion is. My girls and I will attend to his needs."

Crystalyn's hands went to her hips. "He needs the healing of rest. Keep your ministrations and those of your girls to assisting him with it for now. Notify me the moment he's able to speak."

Sabella smiled. "He's with expert care. I'll send one of the girls to inform you the moment he utters a syllable, if he does."

Crystalyn folded her arms at her small waist, staring at the shorter woman. Finally, she gave a brief nod. "See that you do. Come Broth, attend me to our rooms. Hastel, take the first watch outside this one." The soft creaks of four padded feet and the thumps of two booted feet accompanied her as Crystalyn vanished from sight.

Trenton wished he could ask her to stay.

When all was quiet, Sabella sat down, leaning close. "Blink your eyes if you can," she whispered.

Trenton blinked, mildly surprised that he could.

Sabella smiled. "Good man. I have an offer for you. If you choose to accept, close your eyes twice with deliberation. The hooded man will send you where you want to go before daylight wanes for something you possess. He wishes the red crystal. Do you agree?"

Trenton thought about it. He could salvage the mission. Katy would still be waiting. The suit should have the power to contact her left within its cells. He'd save many lives.

The price was steep. Even thinking about the orb made him want to take it out, feel its perfect weight in his palm as he gazed deep into its depths, and bask in the oneness of its bonding. How could he give it away?

People died the longer he was away. Some of those were his friends. He had to make the attempt, though he wasn't at all certain he could go through with it. Slowly and deliberately, he blinked. Twice.

Sabella laughed quietly, her gray eyes merry. "Good. Now, as for me, I require two silver rectangles and... one bell with you before you go. Do you agree?"

Trenton had already agreed to part with something precious. The rest of her request meant little. He nodded. Wait! He felt his head move, albeit minutely. But it had moved.

Sabella's smile was beatific. "That was better than a blink. Let me check and see if it means what I think," she whispered with a soft husky lilt to her voice. Her arm reached low. Sabella giggled. "Yes, your skin is warming."

Trenton took her at her word. He couldn't yet feel her touch, wherever it was, but she had his gratitude. The woman promised to have the connections to get him home.

He knew her type well. Sabella would keep those promises as long as she received something matching her desires.

Chapter Nine

Ascension Gate

Trenton disliked seeing the scarred-faced warrior sitting in a thick-bottomed chair, his leather boots propped up on a wooden table across the hall. On a second wooden table near his elbow, a tankard resided, freshly refilled or still full from the original filling. The grizzled warrior's single blue eye that gazed at the door to his room was alert and glinted with the hardness of promised violence with little provocation.

Trenton drew back from the keyhole and climbed to his feet quietly. Though locked, he'd tested it slowly, and it had made no noise, a fact he was grateful for now. Hastel kept watch for Crystalyn. Thinking about the elegant woman sent a thrill through him, but he had no desire to face her again. True, Crystalyn had saved him from the alien malice invading his mind somehow, but the more he met with her, the harder time he'd have leaving. There was something about her.

A quick look out the only window in the room showed a dead-end alley three stories down. He focused on the window. Built solid inside the window's frame, there was no latch. Removing the glasscutter from the chest pocket of the suit, he made quick work of it, cutting it completely out around the frame. He had no choice but to push on the glass and let it fall, wincing at the loud tinkle of it shattering on the ground.

Trenton waited a few tense heartbeats, but no one came to investigate.

Draping a bath rag over the sill, he backed out on his knees, eased himself over the side, and hung by both hands, once again glad for his grip-enhanced rockprene gloves. Letting go with his right hand, he activated the cutter and melted a handhold on his left and right sides, and then exchanged his grip on the sill.

Testing the hole for the right cooling temperature, Trenton slipped his left hand in the stone. From there, he had no choice but to let his left arm hold his weight as his right hand found the hole he burned. After he had both hands in their new holes, he reached down as far as he could and repeated the process. Trenton worked methodically.

His feet touched the ground a few minutes sooner than he expected. Extinguishing the cutter, he stepped away from the wall and faced the dead end, toward the way out.

A figure stood there, startling him.

"How remarkable," Atoi said. Her green eyes and red lips stood out starkly against her pale skin, and her smooth compassionless face did not match her words. "At first I thought you had used precise control of the Flow, the same as one I know who dribbles the Flow for heating food. Now I have seen it is a device attached to your finger and made to look like one of your digits. Or is it an actual organic part of you?"

Trenton ignored her questioned. "What are you doing here?"

With an object she held in her hand, Atoi pointed at a wooden door leading into the tavern beside her. The long sleeves of her silky black shirt had concealed her dagger. "The back entrances to establishments suit our needs better," she said, her voice taking on the odd echoing quality he'd heard the day before.

Trenton strode past her. "I should ask what you're doing with a dagger and why you need back entrances, but I'm in a bit of a hurry."

Atoi's smaller strides matched his easily, though she didn't look like she had to run. Her feet barely touched the ground. "You are leaving?"

The alley opened onto a back street near to the main one accessing the front of the Quench Quarters. "Yes."

Atoi kept pace as they crossed the major thoroughfare and headed toward the Old Town Coliseum, passing the building where he'd hidden in the shadows and waited for the patrol to dash by.

"Do you not like this world?" Atoi asked abruptly.

As they walked underneath the stern-faced statues, Trenton stole an occasional glance at his young escort, searching for a clue for how to answer in the least offensive way. As they entered the coliseum, he gave up. Her pale, child-like face gave nothing away.

Trenton halted beyond hearing of the short line of people waiting to show their marker. "Your world is for you, mine is for me," he finally replied, happy with its simplicity. Brief replies kept conversations from becoming too complicated. Usually.

"So, you plan to return to your home world."

Trenton gave a brief nod, though the tiny girl hadn't asked a question. Reaching between the folds of his gray robe, he slipped his hand in the front pocket of his suit and clutched at the bronze medallion, his marker to get home. Sabella had given it to him after their early morning liaison. The woman had still insisted upon a second time, though he'd provided her with most of the gold and silver in Khiminay's bag.

Trenton pulled the medallion out and turned it over in his palm. A surprisingly lifelike image of a man's shadowed face cloaked by a hood left only the man's jaws and chin bare. The beaten steel had a depth nearly as detailed as a holo image. He rolled the pendant in his fingers. On the back, beakers filled with liquid, some clear enough to see through, crowded the small area.

"I have traveled to your world for a time. Did you know this?" Atoi asked.

Closing his fist on the medallion, Trenton looked up. "When? How did you get there?"

Atoi blinked. Her face took on an imperious cast. "He may not let you go," she boomed, her voice echoing around him as if coming from a great distance.

"Who might not let me?"

"He Who Watches Worlds."

Her otherworldly voice filled the pit of his stomach with alarm. "Who is 'He?'" he asked, the last nearly a shout.

Atoi regarded him, her smooth face as dispassionate as ever. "Your world has no beauty."

Trenton couldn't argue, nor did he want to bring up the commonplace violence and great malice lurking in her world. He was reluctant to leave, though he wasn't certain why. "I have to go," he said after a time. Searching Atoi's haughty face, he waited for a response.

Atoi said nothing.

Turning away, he strode to an empty podium and handed the marker to the clerk; a woman wearing black armor. The woman glanced at it and then turned to the soldier behind her, handing it to him.

Taking it, the soldier moved to the front of the line, blocking a brown-robed woman and six other patrons from stepping forward. The soldier gestured for Trenton to come forth.

Apparently, the marker had value.

There was no sign of animosity as he passed by those waiting in line ahead of him. Not even from the gray-haired woman wearing the same color of robe as her hair, who stood hunched over second in line.

If anything, man or woman, they all avoided looking at him.

Stepping onto a small brown granite landing beside the soldier, Trenton turned for a last view of Astura.

Atoi had vanished.

Ambling away toward the arched exit of Old Town Coliseum was the odd beast with the wolf's face and feline body he'd last seen beside Crystalyn at the tavern's table, or another like him. Slipping outdoors, the creature hadn't looked in his direction once, but he had a feeling it had likely already reported his whereabouts to the intriguing woman. Trenton knew a moment of regret; he would've liked to become acquainted with her better.

"The ascension gate awaits your use, my lord," the soldier said, the tone of his voice neutral.

Turning his back on where he'd last seen the creature, Trenton cleared it from his mind and took in the topaz gate, the ascension gate as most called it. As high as the stern statues outside in the courtyard, the honey-colored crystal spanned much of the distance from the smooth granite floor to the oblong domed roof cut from the same quarry.

Near the top of the obelisks, two symbols shaped as interlocking chain links, making up a circle, rotated slowly. Yet, the most abnormal aspect of the obelisks occurred between them.

A misty opaque curtain of darkness spun in a constant flux gripped in a churning maelstrom, as if the fabric of reality had folded into a black hole to another dimension.

Going through the dark curtain would mean returning to radiation storms and the dark things swooping and clawing out of them. But it was home, a world where he belonged.

Taking a deep breath, Trenton strode into the mist.

ALSO BY R.V. JOHNSON

The Flow of Power Chronicles:
Beyond the Sapphire Gate
Beyond the Dark Gate
Beyond Astura
Beyond High Reach

R.V. Johnson has had the worlds of the *Beyond* series hovering in his thoughts for many seasons. *Beyond Terra* slipped in while writing *Beyond the Sapphire Gate*, and *Beyond the Dark Gate*.
The author and publisher appreciate reviews of your enjoyment of this novella. Please leave one.

R.V. Johnson grew up in Utah wandering through beautiful tranquil forests, exploring the unique alien-like setting of the red rock desert, and climbing the rugged trails of the high Uinta Mountains where moun-

tain goats roam. Indoors, he read from his extensive library, or wrote in his journal. One can now find him writing and reading outside.
He strives to be the gem the dragon hoards.
https://www.authorrvjohnson.com

www.ingramcontent.com/pod-product-compliance
Lightning Source LLC
Chambersburg PA
CBHW032252070726
47590CB00016B/2573